Blood Red Ochre

BLOOD RED OCHRE

Kevin Major

Delacorte Press/New York
Doubleday Canada Limited/Toronto

Canadian Cataloguing in Publication Data

Major, Kevin, 1949-
  Blood red ochre

ISBN 0-385-29794-7

1. Beothuk Indians – Juvenile fiction. 2. Indians of North America – Newfoundland – Juvenile Fiction. I. Title.

PS8576.A36B56 1989   JC813'.54   C88-094187-1 PZ7.M34B1 1989

Library of Congress Cataloging in Publication Data
Major, Kevin.
    Blood red ochre/Kevin Major.
        p. cm.
    Summary: Living in Newfoundland, fifteen-year-old David meets a mysterious new girl named Nancy and makes a startling discovery while doing research for a school project on the Beothuk Indians.
    ISBN 0-385-29794-7
    1. Beothuk Indians – Juvenile fiction. [1. Beothuk Indians – Fiction. 2. Indians of North America – Newfoundland – Fiction. 3. Newfoundland – Fiction] I. Title.
    PZ7.M28B1 1989
    [Fic] – dc19

Published in Canada by
Doubleday Canada Limited
105 Bond Street
Toronto, Ontario
M5B 1Y3

Published in the United States by Delacorte Press
Bantam Doubleday Dell Publishing Group, Inc.
666 Fifth Avenue
New York, NY
10103

The author acknowledges with gratitude The Canada Council for its assistance during the writing of this book, and John Hewson and Ralph Pastore of Memorial University for their valuable comments on Dauoodaset's story.

Printed in Canada.

To the memory of my mother and father

David

"So what?" he said, then waited a few seconds. "Ah, you'd be bored out of your mind if things were perfect all the time." He laughed a bit.

When David looked across the front seat at his mother, he could see that she didn't think it was so funny. He'd said things to her in the past few weeks that he never would have dreamed of saying before. Even when he softened them up with a few wisecracks, she still wasn't able to deal with it.

"Don't get me wrong. It's not that I don't like him," he added.

He glanced at her again. She continued to stare out the window, the same deadly serious look on her face. He couldn't make up his mind if it was because of the snow beating wildly against the windshield. He knew how much she hated winter driving, even though the pickup was four-wheel drive.

"If they had any sense they'd cancel school, weather like this," he said, hoping to get her mind onto something else.

"Be honest, David, do that much at least."

He knew now he'd better try something different.

"You know yourself he takes things too far sometimes,"

1

he said sharply, thinking the bit of anger in his voice might settle it all.

There was no change in her expression.

"We put up with each other," he said, sounding more serious this time.

She sighed. "That's about it."

"There you go—taking his side again."

"I'm not taking anybody's side," she said.

That's just it, he felt like saying. Anytime he had an argument with him, all she ever wanted to do was keep the peace between them, rather than face up to who was right and who was wrong.

"You're at that age," she said.

God, he hated it, the way she passed things off like that! He forced his teeth hard against each other to keep from saying anything.

She turned up the speed of the wiper blades. Then she turned it down again because of the loud slapping against the ice on the edge of the windshield.

The pickup stopped at the access road which led up to the school. She turned and gave him a thin smile. "Your father's not so bad. You got to give him a chance."

He opened the door and got out.

"See you lunchtime," she said, almost like nothing out of the ordinary had passed between them.

"Whose father?" he said.

He shut the door hard before she had a chance to say anything else.

He started running. When he reached the main entrance of the school, he looked back. The pickup had only just started to turn back onto the road.

He pulled the door open and went inside. The first bell of the morning had rung already. The corridors were almost empty as he strolled to his locker. He hung up his coat and changed into sneakers.

"He's marking the register," one of the other students from his grade ten class said, running past him toward the classroom, the laces of her sneakers untied.

He wasn't going to rush it. He casually checked the timetable taped on the inside of his locker door. Math the first period. He worked his way through the pile of books and came up with his algebra text, an exercise book stuck between the pages.

He bent down to pick up a pen which had rolled out of the locker and dropped to the floor. From around his neck fell a pendant on a leather thong. It was flat and made of bone, with a pattern of fine reddish markings on one side. Its shape reminded him of the wing of a bird.

It had been given to him years ago by his grandfather. He had told David it was a Beothuk Indian pendant his own grandfather had given to him as a boy. He had warned him not to tell anybody about it because by law anything like that was supposed to have been turned over to the government.

Why David had decided to string a piece of leather through it the night before and start wearing it, he wasn't really sure. The Beothuks were extinct, and there wasn't a great deal that was known about them. He knew his wearing the pendant had something to do with his own feeling of having a past that he didn't know much about. And something to do with keeping a secret that would always be only his.

He dropped the pendant inside his sweatshirt and did up two of its three buttons.

The classroom door was closed by the time he got there. He opened it slowly and found everybody standing at their desks, waiting for the national anthem to play over the intercom. Dalton, the homeroom teacher, stared at him.

"I missed the bus."

"Wait outside."

He closed the door again. He stood leaning against the wall, looking vacantly down the corridor, until the music was over and Dalton came out.

"This is the second time in a week. Once more and I'll be reporting you to the office."

David didn't say anything. He saw Mrs. Baker, the math teacher, coming and he stepped out of the way to let her into the classroom.

"I corrected the Heritage 1200 papers last night," Dalton said. "Fifty-four percent. That's not like you. That's down almost thirty marks from your last assignment. What's up?"

"Nothing."

"There's got to be something."

David shrugged and looked away.

"I'm not the only teacher complaining about you."

Still no reaction.

"Okay, have it your way. But if this keeps up I'll be calling your parents." Dalton walked away.

David went inside and sat in his seat, the first one in the second row. The others had already started their math. He opened his textbook and found the page where he had been working the last period. He had almost finished the chapter on polynomials, but he didn't feel much like writing the test. He was making his way through the chapter review and stretching it out as long as he could.

He turned around and started to torment Julie about her hair. She'd had it cut the day before. He told her it looked like she'd had a fight with a lawnmower.

"Very original," she said, sneering.

Just then he caught sight of someone new in the classroom — a girl in the next row, three seats from the back. It took him by surprise. He stared at her.

She had roughly cut, black hair and a dark complexion.

When she looked up and he saw her face, he felt a rush inside him. She looked different, foreign almost, a bit mysterious. He could hardly take his eyes off her.

"Who's that?" he whispered to Julie.

She wouldn't answer.

"C'mon."

"Apologize first."

He just grinned.

"You're going to get it."

"Promise?"

Julie took a swipe at him with her calculator. He jerked back in his seat.

"David . . . " It was Mrs. Baker.

He turned back to his math slowly, at the same time taking another long look at the new girl. She looked up again and then directly at him. Her eyes too were black, and deeply serious. Was there a hint of a smile? Was she remembering him from somewhere? He couldn't think where.

He bent over his desk, to make it look as if he was hard at work. He searched his brain trying to figure out if he had seen her before. He gave up. Then, turning his head only slightly, he called under his breath to the guy across from him in the next row. "Jim, who is she?" He pointed his thumb in the general direction of the seats behind him.

"Wha'?"

"Get your ears checked. The new girl. What's her name?"

Jim shrugged and went back to the problem he'd been working on.

"Get your hormones checked while you're at it."

Jim gave him the finger.

He tried Julie again.

"It's Nancy," she said, finally. "Now quit bothering me."

He could see Mrs. Baker looking at him again. He went back to his work.

Nancy, he thought. But he still couldn't remember knowing her from anywhere. He wondered where she was living.

During recess he managed to find out only that one thing. She was staying in one of the old places on Spencer's Bank. He couldn't remember people living in either one of those houses anymore except in the summertime.

He saw her lingering for a while in the corridor by herself. He was tempted to go up and talk to her, but he wasn't sure how well that would come off.

He hung around his locker, trying to keep to himself. Jim was bugging him about his plans for the weekend.

"Wanna go ice fishing?"

He shrugged.

"I can get Dad's Ski-doo."

"So."

"Man, you're weird," Jim said finally. "You never want to do anything anymore."

David ignored him. Later, on the way home for lunch, he made it a point not to sit with him on the bus. He sat by himself.

There were just the three of them for lunch — himself and his mother, and Sandra, his ten-year-old sister. Brad, who was a year and a half younger than David, had stayed in school for a floor hockey game. The old man was gone for all day cutting wood.

His mother had made hamburgers and french fries. She was being particularly nice to him for some reason. He figured it was probably guilt.

He hardly said two words during the whole meal. She was complaining again about the fact that he would never tell her anything about what went on at school. The school could burn to the ground, she joked, and she'd have to find out from someone else. It was hardly enough to get a smile from him.

It was weird, he was thinking. Up to a few weeks before, he had never really thought of her as anybody but his mother — the one who was usually there in the house when he got home from school, who provided the meals and worried about him for no good reason. He never really thought about her as someone with a personality, with good points and bad ones. He never really looked at her like he did other people, like a teacher or something.

The fact was she had been a teacher herself at one time. It was years ago when teachers were in short supply in Newfoundland, when a year of university was enough to get a job. Before he was born, she gave it up. Some of the people she taught with had gone back to university to finish their degrees. She never did. And the time came when she couldn't even qualify to substitute for a day when one of the regular teachers got sick.

Lately he'd been wondering about that. Maybe the work she did on all those committees didn't really satisfy her. Maybe she really wanted to be doing something else, a paying job or something.

He had been wondering most of all about how much he was the reason for her getting married. Last month he had found out that the man she did get married to was not his father.

He had been doing an assignment for Heritage 1200 on tracing ancestors. He had kept asking questions he couldn't get any straight answers to, when she called him aside in the bedroom.

She was upset and she wasn't hiding it very well. Then she came out with it — that his father was really someone else, someone she didn't want to marry and who was married himself now and living in St. John's.

He didn't know what to do. He stared at her, hardly able

to believe it. For a minute he thought he was going to cry or something. He was too stunned to do anything.

When he held on, stiff and trying to act as if it wasn't really hurting him, she took his head in her hands and kissed him.

Then she said, "You're the reason I gave up work."

Now he knew the truth was she would have lost her job anyway.

"I got no regrets," she said to him. "I loved you too much for that."

He believed that. He really had to believe that much.

He wasn't over it yet. He was still mad at them for keeping it from him for so long. He'd found out since that other people, including some of his friends, had known about it all along.

When he looked across the kitchen table now, he was giving her the message that making hamburgers and french fries was not going to do much to change the mood he was in.

He left the house early to walk the mile and a half back to school instead of taking the bus. It was still snowing, but the wind had died out. He had his Walkman with him, the headphones under the hood of his parka. He turned up the music so loud that there was nothing else he could hear.

At school that afternoon he stuck to himself. Julie asked him if he was sick or something.

The last period in the afternoon was heritage class. Except for that one assignment he'd been getting good marks all year. He thought of it as one of the subjects he was really interested in.

Dalton set the last assignment for the term, a research .paper, at least two thousand words. He gave them two weeks to hand in an outline and six weeks to have in the final draft. It was going to be worth fifteen percent of the year's mark. He told them it could be on a topic of their own choosing, as long as it expanded on something they had discussed in the course during the year.

Between the final bell and the time his bus left, he made a quick trip to the library. He thought maybe he'd get some books for the assignment before they were all checked out. He had decided to do it on the Beothuks. Shanawdithit, the last one, died in 1829. And her grave had been lost during the construction of a new street in St. John's. That much he remembered from when they had talked about them in class. He knew more of it would come back to him once he started reading the books.

Mrs. Sinclair, the librarian, was sitting at the checkout desk. He asked her for help finding some books. She faked a look of irritation and said to look in the card catalogue, that was what it was there for. He complained that he didn't have the time, and he might end up missing the bus. She grinned and tried to look like she wouldn't give in, but then she pointed to the stacks in the back of the room. "Second last one on the right," she said, "third shelf from the bottom." She turned back to what she had been doing before he interrupted her.

His eyes ran over the titles on the shelf until he came to one that caught his attention — *The Beothuks or Red Indians* by James P. Howley. He took it out and then found a couple more that had the word "Beothuk" in the titles.

He straightened up and headed toward the checkout desk. Then he caught sight of Nancy. She was sitting in one of the study cubicles, writing in a notebook. She looked up, but didn't show much interest in his being there. He smiled and slowed down a bit, without really stopping.

"Getting some books for the assignment," he said. "On the Beothuks." He held one of them up as if he needed to prove it.

She stared at him, then smiled. It was definitely a smile.

By that time he was past her and almost at the checkout desk, walking sideways and still smiling himself. He had decided he couldn't really stop and go back. Anyway, he didn't want her to think he was being pushy.

"Don't rush yourself now. I'm sure the bus will wait," Mrs. Sinclair said, her voice full of sarcasm.

Nancy's face suddenly turned serious.

"Right," he said, caught off balance by the change in Nancy's expression. He turned the rest of the way around and gave Mrs. Sinclair the books.

When she had finished with them, he headed for the door. As he was leaving he turned back for a last look at Nancy. But the cubicle was empty and there was no sign of her anywhere.

Aboard the bus, he sat by himself again. He put on the headphones. He sat with U2 blasting in his ears, thinking of Nancy, and looking at the pictures in Howley's book on the Beothuks.

Dauoodaset

It is winter still. Seven of our people came many days over land from the great lake. We wait in this place by the river until the ice melts into pieces to run down to the saltwater. We will go with the running water to find salmon and the beaches heavy with mussels at the drawing down of the tide. There will be seals thick with fat and many seabirds for our arrows. We will not hunger. Spring will be a new life for our people.

I tell Waumaduit, my mother, that the caribou meat in our storehouse will keep us strong until we make the journey. She looks at me with sorrow in her eyes.

"The winter cold will be long. Our caribou meat will not last," she says.

"I do not need meat today," I say to her. I give her a laugh. "Rest in winter, like the beaver."

Still my mother's lips do not smile. She is a good woman, but she worries hard. It is not good to worry hard. It makes more pain.

We made our storehouse in the fall when we came to this place by the river. Made of poles, strong together, tied hard with roots. In the fall the wind blew in and dried the meat of the caribou. When it rained we covered the sticks of our storehouse with skin of the birch trees. Now the meat is hard with frost.

It is true, our kill of caribou was small. Not enough hunters among us to make a long caribou fence. Not enough hunters to drive into the fence all the caribou that ran by. I killed two—my best spear sank into the necks so hard the point of the spear came out the other side. Dark blood soaked the moss. My uncle talked, "Bloody moss kill! Dauoodaset made bloody moss kill!" Pride filled up my heart. I am a hunter now who made the same kills as my father.

I go now to the storehouse for meat for Waumaduit to cook. She waits at the fire with the cooking pots. Stones lie red hot in the fire. Young Shamoonon brings clean snow to melt for water. In the storehouse I choose a piece with bone. I will have bone and others will have meat. It is enough for me. It is not me who will go hunting today.

The stones heat the water and make it bubble in the cooking pots. My mother makes very strong cooking pots from skin of birch trees. We have many of them. My father tells her there is no need for so many. She wants to keep working, as in the days before, she says to him. Perhaps one day we will need them. She does not cry when she says this to him.

My uncle, Edeshnon, the chief, and my other uncle, Cosheewet, come back without a kill today. No one says they are sorry, no one is surprised. It is like the day before, and before. We talk inside the mamateek, around the fire. They saw tracks of a marten, new tracks, but they were hard to follow on the ice of the river. Tomorrow I will hunt for food. Maybe I will come back with a kill.

There is some laughter in the talk of Abideshet, my father, and my uncles. They remember the kills of many caribou, the joy of many feasts. We were seven mamateeks then, when I was born. There was dancing and singing and eating of seabirds and beaver. Again there will be dancing and singing, in the spring when we camp by the saltwater. There will be no whiteman there to bother us. We have traveled far away from the whiteman, I say to them. This is new land. It will be our land. We will grow strong in it, Abideshet. He is happy that I talk like a man with fire in my spirit. Waumaduit says I am too fearless when I talk. Remember your grandfather, she says, he talked with fire. Now he lies in the ground, dead by the gun.

I remember him. But my people will not grow to be strong again on memories. To myself I say this. We will be again what our people were. We will have strength and spread our people across the land.

I remember Shanawdithit. She stayed with her people by the great lake. She would not leave her sick family to come with us to this river. She will wait and one day she will be my wife. We will be together and we will have children so our people will grow to be many again. It is long that we wait. I think of her all the days since we have left her people.

Our talk is not long in the mamateek tonight. Remembering makes our people quiet. Now we lie with our own thinking, not the talk of others. No baby cries to break our quiet, only the cough of Baethasuit to make it long. Baethasuit, my uncle's wife, has coughed for many days. It will not go away. It is time to build a sweathouse, my uncle says. She will grow weaker and it will be hard to make our journey. Cosheewet fears for his wife. We have seen this whiteman's cough kill many of our people.

I must mend one of my snowshoes for tomorrow's hunt. It will take my thoughts away from Shanawdithit and stop the stirrings in my body. I ache to have her near me. Be patient, my father has said to me when we were alone. He smiles at my wanting. I know grandchildren would make him happy. A girl child he says, there will be a girl child for your mother to forget her sorrow. A child to grow and make children.

I rise from the warmth of the caribou fur and go quietly to the wall of mamateek, to where my snowshoes hang. I sit with the one that needs repair, at the end of my resting pit, near to the fire. I put sticks on the fire to give more light for my work.

A glow of light spreads over those who sleep. Only the form of Baethasuit moves, her covering of caribou skin rising with her coughs. She lies alone, empty resting pits on each side of her. Edeshnon, the noisy one, drones like an old bear.

I follow the smoke rising straight up from the fire. It is drawn away through the hole in the peak of the mamateek, out into the night sky. I turn my head and I can see stars through the hole. Clear night, perhaps clear day tomorrow.

Waumaduit has cut new strips of caribou hide for me. I take two strips and soak them in water. With the edge of my knife I cut away the frayed strips from my snowshoe. I tie a new piece to the front crosswood and weave it through to the crosswood at the bottom. I make a strong knot and cut away the end. I do this a second time.

When I finish my work I rest the snowshoe near the fire to dry the strips of hide. Not too close. Too much heat will make them brittle. In the morning they will be tight and strong for my hunting.

I lie back in the furs of my resting pit and take off silently the mantle of fur I have worn for many days. Waumaduit has warned that our caribou sleeping furs are few. We must use the mantles of day to keep us warm at night. But it is good to lie naked with only the loose spread of fur over my body. I think of the days of summer when there is no need for heavy coverings. I remember the rushing waters of streams splashing against us.

Shanawdithit, in our young days, would hide in the bushes near the streams and call to me, teasing me. I would chase her into the water, but she swam like an otter. I could catch her only when she let me. And then she would slip away again. We were children. I think now of her, not as a child, but as a woman splashing in the water of the streams.

David

When David came indoors late that afternoon the first person he saw was the old man. He was sitting in one of the armchairs in the living room, his feet in heavy wool socks on the coffee table, his head back. There were bits of sawdust still in his hair. He looked like he was asleep. He'd left the house early that morning, before David had gotten up to get ready for school.

David followed the smell of macaroni and cheese into the kitchen.

"Another twenty minutes," his mother said before he had a chance to ask.

He searched the cupboards until he came up with a few chocolate cookies to hold him over. He could feel her looking at him.

"Now, don't spoil your supper."

He left again without saying anything to her. In the living room he sat down in the armchair closest to the TV. It was almost five thirty. Good timing. He hadn't missed any of the show he usually watched.

Sandra and Brad were on the sofa, each one complaining that the other was taking up too much space.

"So, how many goals you score?" David asked his brother.

"None."

"Slack."

"I got two assists."

"Got lucky again?"

Brad screwed up his face at him. David gave him a long fake grin. He liked to rub it in when Brad didn't play as well as he usually did.

When the show started he told them to quit their fooling around. "Go to your own rooms somewhere."

They ignored him and continued flicking at each other. Quietly at first, but then suddenly a lot louder.

"Will you guys shut up for once!" he yelled at them.

That brought their father straight up in his chair. "What the hell is goin' on? Can't anyone get five minutes rest around here."

"It's David," Brad said.

"It was not me. You're the ones makin' the racket."

"You're the one who yelled."

"I was only tryin' to get you two to shut up. How can anyone listen to TV the way you guys are carrying on?"

The old man glared at him. "You didn't have to scream at them. They're not deaf."

"Sure, blame it all on me, why don't ya."

"I'm not blamin' it all on you."

"Sure sounds like it."

"David, shut it up right now. And don't be so bloody hard to get along with."

He felt like getting up and taking off out of the room. But he knew the old man would accuse him of sulking if he did. "Can't even watch TV around here," he mumbled to himself and turned back to the screen.

It was really getting to him. His mother had said it was

worse since he'd found out. She said he'd changed. But he didn't buy that. What changed, to his mind, was the guilt he used to feel over the fact that there was a lot about the old man that he could never take to. That guilt was gone. And for good reason, he kept telling himself.

He remembered once, when he was twelve, he went along with him moose hunting for a weekend. They had gone in the woods together a few times when he was younger. The old man showed him what he knew about snaring rabbits and shooting partridge, until he had grown old enough that when he did feel like going in the woods, he went instead with Jim and other fellows his own age.

Moose hunting was all the old man thought about in the fall of the year. Every September, never fail, he took a week for a trip with one of his friends into Western Ridge "to get his moose." If his name wasn't drawn for a license, he went anyway, to be the cook for some fellows who did have licenses. Or so he said. David could never remember a winter without a deep freeze full of moose steaks and "moose burger," as the old man liked to call it.

Moose hunting is generally a man's sport, not a young fellow's. Even so, the old man wanted him to go along for the weekend—from Friday night to Sunday, when he'd have to be back home for school the next day. They left the house with the camper on the pickup, loaded with supplies. They stopped to pick up his hunting buddy and made a trip to the liquor store along the way for a couple bottles of black rum.

There was no special treatment for him. They tramped through the woods most of Saturday, stopping only for lunches now and then. They kept at it even when it started to rain. By the time they got back to the camper, he was drenched to the skin, exhausted, and cold, aching from having walked so far. They hadn't even seen any fresh tracks.

They got back just as it was getting dark. All he wanted to do was get out of his wet clothes and get into something dry and warm.

"Here," the old man said, handing him an open bottle of rum. "Take a glutch o' that. That'll soon warm ya up."

He did what he said, swallowing almost a mouthful of the stuff. It burnt a path down his throat until he started to choke, half of it sputtering back up. He coughed and coughed.

It started the old man laughing. He stopped all of a sudden when David threw up his guts on the floor in front of him.

"You all right?"

When he looked up, a grin spread across the old man's face. David started to cry.

"C'mon, c'mon, enough o' that." When he didn't stop, the old man said to him, "Now, don't be so childish." He was embarrassed in front of his hunting buddy.

After a time he tried to help him out of his wet clothes. David pushed him away.

"Okay, okay." The old man cleaned up the mess. Then he sat back at the table and they started to drink. They kept at it until both of them passed out in their bunks.

David had lain there in his own bunk the whole time, pretending he was asleep, dying to go to the can. Only after he was sure they weren't going to move did he get up and go outside.

He went for weeks after that feeling really mad inside about what happened. Now it wasn't the big deal that it was then, since he'd started having a beer once in a while with the fellows. But it was still the thing that came to his mind first whenever he thought about why they didn't get along.

His mother called them for supper. During the meal, when Brad and his father were talking about the snowmobile and why it was so hard to get started, David didn't say anything, even though he figured he knew just as much as Brad did about what was wrong with it.

Instead, he asked his mother if she knew anything about the Beothuks, just so that it didn't look like he was any quieter than he usually was.

"I've heard your grandfather talk about someplace where they used to live. Don't ask me where. Maybe your father knows."

"Knows what?" the old man asked.

"Never mind," David said.

The old man didn't take it any further. David wasn't surprised. He knew he was more interested in the Ski-doo and in Brad.

He went into his room after supper and stayed there most of the evening. It wasn't like him to be spending so much time by himself. But it was better, he figured, than trying to be nice to them when he didn't feel like it. At least he was being honest.

Jim phoned to ask him something about the French homework they had to do. What he really wanted to talk about were his plans for the weekend. David just let him talk, not saying much himself. After a while he lied to get him off the phone, telling him that his mother wanted to use it.

He was in a rotten mood. He kept thinking how he'd like to be someplace where no one knew who he was. Perhaps that was why Nancy was so much on his mind. She was someone different who didn't know anything about him.

He went to bed with Howley's book on the Beothuks. He had found out that it was a reprint of a book first published in 1915. The book was over 350 pages long and the print was small. He tried reading it from the beginning, but he soon started skipping pages. He stopped a few times where it mentioned Beothuks being killed or when a picture caught his eye.

After a while he was finding it harder and harder to concentrate. He kept thinking of Nancy and what had happened that day in the library. The book eventually fell to his lap.

He went over every word he had spoken to her. What she said and the way she said it. How she looked and the way he remembered he looked at her.

More than anything he wondered what she thought of him. She seemed friendly enough in the library. At first, anyway. He really didn't know, did he?

The only thing he had decided before falling asleep was that he would have to come up with some way of getting to know her better. And to do it without looking stupid or ending up with the other fellows in the class making cracks about it in front of her. It was hard to figure out just what the best move would be.

Dauoodaset

The cold makes me stir. It is the earliest light of morning. Silently, beneath the furs of my resting pit, I cover myself again with the fur of my body mantle and rise up. I keep the bedding fur wrapped around me still. Only a thin line of smoke rises from the fire pit. I lean ahead to feel the new strips of hide on the snowshoe. They are dry and tight, making it like a new one.

Leaning into the fire pit, I spread apart the ash to find the cinders that make the smoke. At the edge of the fire pit are tiny tearings of birch bark. I scatter a few over the cinders and blow gently upon them. They catch the fire. Quickly I add some small sticks and the red-needled branch of a dead spruce tree.

The first crackling stirs my mother. "Dauoodaset," she whispers. "Put the stones to heat for the boiling pot. You cannot go without hot drink. I will steep some leaves."

My plan was to slip away before the others awaken, but now I must do as Waumaduit asks. Sometimes she treats me as a child, not as a man. It does not go well with me, but I must not think of that. She has much to worry her. We must not bring strong words between us. I know in my mind what I am and what I will be to my people. My father knows how I feel. Sometimes he looks with pity on Waumaduit, and I must do the same.

The sharp taste of the drink takes all the sleep from me. As I sit and drink, the other hunters of our people tell me, "Do not travel far. You do not have the strength to fight wind and snow if it begins to storm. Watch the sky. Take warning with the changes of the clouds. Listen to the voice of the wind."

"Luck to you, Dauoodaset. May the spirits watch over you and give you of their store." They are the words we always say to hunters.

I leave with the good wishes of my people said louder than sounds true. They do not believe I will have such good fortune. That is why I wished to go silently, without them watching me go.

For a while I follow yesterday's footprints of my uncles. The snowshoes scrape the crust of old broken snow. I travel fast and with too much noise. I remember now to go slow and save my strength for when it is needed most.

I stop and look about me. Even with all the wanting in my body I see still the beauty of this land. Long tree shadows stretch themselves upon the snow. Where the early sun catches the flakes of snow it sparkles like the rain on spruce needles in the days of summer. There is no sound, only that of a faraway tree bird. My people were wise to come to this land. It has the stillness of happy spirits. It has the breath of a land where no whiteman has been.

I start again along the bank of the river past where my uncles turned into the woods. When I make my place of turning it is where the land starts to grow steep. My uncles thought it better than to use their strength on this climb. But it is not as hard as first it looks. The snowshoes do not break the crust or slip back. I go around the hill to where the sun shines strongest.

It is time to rest again. I slip away one of the snowshoes from my foot for a place to sit. It is good to feel the sun bright against my face. Its heatlight takes the chill from my bones. The sun will grow stronger when it rises higher in the morning sky.

While I rest I check the tightness of my bowstring. The warming air has not loosened it. This bow is of my own making, strong ash wood, almost the length of me. It has made no killings yet, but it is ready. I have worked many hours to make it. Animal grease has kept it keen and ready. My first bow I have given to Shamoonon, my cousin. He has not grown enough to hold it well, but it makes for him a good practice bow.

My arrows too I check, but there is no need. They are light and straight and ready to do their killing. One, a present from my father, has killed six times. Four by him and two jays by me. It is the first bird arrow I would choose. There is an old saying of my people — arrow stained with blood knows the smell of meat.

I use the other snowshoe to dig away the snow beneath the spruce tree near where I sit. My father taught me this when I was a small child. Today I have much luck. There are berries, thick in the moss since the time snow first began to fall. They are dark red and in my mouth they burst with their frosty juice. It is the best taste I have had for many days. I quickly scrape the snow for more.

But suddenly I stop. My body holds itself still and I keep my breath inside me. I have heard the flutter of wings. There are partridge in the woods near where I sit.

Slowly I turn, and crouch low on my snowshoes. Quietly, quietly I slip the straps of hide about my feet. One hand reaches for the bow, which lies upon the snow; the other chooses two bird arrows from the pouch near it. The tips of the bird arrows are blunt so they will not damage any of the precious meat.

Now I see them. Two partridge at the edge of a thick

clump of alder trees. Hard to see, their feathers are the color of shaded snow. And now they see me. I rise slowly, and at the same time I am setting one of the arrows against the bow and drawing back its feathered end and the string together. I know that this may be my best chance.

Just as I am ready to shoot, the birds begin to move away. I take my aim just above them and snap the arrow into its flight. One bird flutters up as if to meet the arrow. The arrow hits with a thud in the head, dropping it back to the ground. The other bird is gone.

Quickly I race to where the bird lies upon the snow. I grab it and twist the neck to be sure that it will not come to life again. It is now that I feel the gladness and the pride of the kill.

The other bird is not for me to see. But I think it has not gone far. I lie low against a birch tree and wait in silence. After a long while I hear its low bird sound. There, I can see tail feathers in the needles of the branches not far away. But it is gone before I have the chance to raise my bow. I creep my way to the trees, but there is no sign of the bird, only its tracks in the white of the snow. I follow them. The strong sun gives each thin lines of shadow.

Then, ahead of me I see the flutter of the bird deep among the trees. There is no chance now of making another partridge kill. The trees where it has gone are too thick. It would be too hard with my long bow.

I rest again. Then walk slowly back to where my partridge lies dead. I come to where it should be, but I am confused and filled with hurt. My arrow lies alone on the snow. Where is the bird that I have killed? Have the spirits taken back their store?

My eyes follow marks upon the snow. They are the marks of something that was dragged. My eyes search the land. In the distance I see the dead bird, and ahead of it, dragging it, a marten!

Quickly as I can I get to my pouch of arrows and ready

my bow for a shot. But the distance to the marten is too great. It would be a waste of a shot. I must gain on the marten if I am to have a chance of a kill. I take long strides toward it with the hope that it will not give up its prize and race away. I am lucky. The marten I think is as hungry as its hunter.

I gain much ground on him. Then, when he sees danger for him getting too near, he drops the bird from his mouth and races across the open snow.

He is too late. The arrow leaves my bow, quick like the lightning through the air. Its sharp point sinks into the leg flesh of the marten. The arrow has smelled meat.

I race to the wounded animal. With its front paws it drags the rest of its body and the arrow. I stop its struggle with the tramp of my snowshoe over its body. It sinks into the snow, snarling, fighting wildly to get away. Its teeth cut at the hide strips of my snowshoe. With my bare hands I push the point of another arrow through its neck and into its skull.

The snow is bloody red. I fall down to the snow, tired and worn and thinking of the joy my meat will bring to our camp.

David

When he woke up in the morning he felt dragged out, like he hadn't had enough sleep. Thoughts about Nancy were still mixing around in his head. She was on his mind all the while he was getting dressed and eating his breakfast.

By the time he reached school all his thinking about her had built up so much that he stayed at the other end of the corridor, away from the classroom, because he was sure he would run into her and not know what to say. When the first bell rang he slipped into the washroom and stayed there until the corridor was almost empty. He strolled into the classroom just as the second bell went. Dalton looked at him, but didn't say anything. David took his seat, glancing at Nancy just long enough to be sure that she was there.

He didn't say much to anyone during the two periods until recess, even though he wasn't really concentrating on his work. He was thinking that at any time she could be looking his way. Even between periods, when Jim tried to get him worked up about the Oilers losing their hockey game the night before, he didn't show much interest. There were only two things he really had on his mind — how to go about setting up a situation where he and Nancy would talk, and what to say to her if he did.

When the recess bell rang he stayed in his seat, making it look like he was finishing up the literature questions the teacher had set the period before. He kept at them until finally Jim gave up waiting for him to go down to the common room.

He had kept his eye on the door all the time he was sitting there. Finally, when it seemed most people had gone and there was quiet in the room, he glanced behind. She was still in her seat, reading. But so were two other people, in other rows, close enough that they would hear anything he might say to her.

He wasn't sure what he should do. Forget it and wait for a better chance? How long would he have to wait? He figured he should at least say something, even if it was only a few words, if all it did was make it easier the next time.

He closed his literature book noisily and stood up. He started walking toward the door. He casually glanced in her direction. She was looking at him. He stopped, like he was noticing for the first time that there was anyone else in the room. He walked down between the seats toward her. He stopped and sat on the desk across from hers, his back to the other people in the room.

"Hi. Started your heritage assignment?"

"I have most of it done," she said.

"You're not serious?"

"I did it last night."

"You don't waste time."

She looked directly at him. "Time is something I've learned not to waste."

It seemed such an odd thing to say. And she said it so seriously, he hardly knew what to do. He smiled awkwardly and put his feet back on the floor. Maybe she didn't want him around?

Then a trace of a smile showed on her face.

"What's your topic?" he asked lamely.

"The same as yours."

"That's a coincidence. The fact that we both chose the same one. Think it means anything?"

He said it just for something to say, not meaning anything by it. When she stared at him with that same serious look, he had to look away.

"I better go," he said. "I want to get something from the canteen."

As he was walking back up between the seats, anxious to get out of the classroom, she called out to him. "We should get together. I might be able to help you out." When he looked back, there was that bit of a smile again.

"Sure," he said.

"Really."

"Okay, sure," he said, trying to sound a bit more excited.

"We can talk about it later."

He weaved his way through the crowds of students in the corridor, puzzled by it all. The way she said things — it wasn't anything like the way he'd been used to girls talking to him.

He had somehow managed to do what he'd set out to do — they had talked and now they had reason to talk again. But he wasn't so certain anymore if that was what he wanted. He just couldn't be sure if she really liked him. In fact, when he thought about it, he couldn't be sure of anything about her. She was really different, that was the only thing.

Maybe that was why now he could feel himself getting more and more interested in her, almost against his will.

She'd sent him stumbling for something to say and then pulled him back each time. It was in her eyes, the way she looked at him. It was her eyes that he really liked. He loved the way she looked at him sometimes.

Loved. It was the first time he felt bold enough to think of it like that.

They met again after school. On Tuesdays he and Jim and some others usually stayed behind in the gym and worked out in the weight room. He told Jim he would be late, and then he got lost in the crowd and went to the library.

Mrs. Sinclair looked surprised to see him. "No big rush today?" she said, smiling.

He didn't say anything, just grinned and walked to the magazine display. He took down a copy of *Music Express* and started flipping through it. He looked up from time to time, when other students drifted into the room.

When Nancy came through the door, his eyes followed her to the same cubicle she'd been sitting in the day before. After she'd been there for a few minutes, he quietly put the magazine back on the shelf and strolled over to her.

"Hi," he said. "Whadaya up to?"

As soon as he said it he knew it sounded ridiculous. It was something he'd say to any other girl, but saying it to her didn't seem right.

"Busy, are you?" he added quickly.

"No, that's okay. Bring over a chair. We can talk."

He pulled over a chair from a study table nearby and sat on it backward, close, but not too close, to her.

"So," he said, "how are you liking it? This school, I mean."

"Like I expected."

"Much different from where you came from?"

She shrugged.

"Where did you come from anyway?"

"It's hard to explain."

He obviously wasn't going to get very far with that, so he decided he'd better get right to the reason they were together before things got messed up again.

"I've made a start on the assignment. I've read parts of those books I checked out. But I'm really mixed up. None of them agree with each other."

"What don't you understand?"

"Well, like how many really got killed off by the settlers, how many died of disease. The books all say different things."

"What do you think?"

"Hell, I don't know."

"Do you care?"

"I suppose. I want to get a half decent mark."

"Is that all you're doing it for?"

"I guess I . . . "

Suddenly, without any warning, she shut all the books in front of her and stood up.

"I have to go. When you get really interested in what you're doing, then we can get together. I don't have the time to spend with you if you're only interested in it for the marks."

"Wait a minute."

She looked straight at him with her dark, angry eyes. "Yes?"

"I didn't mean anything by that. I am interested."

"In me or in the assignment?"

"Both."

"Be honest."

"I *am* being honest. It's just kinda strange, that's all. You're not like other girls."

Someone at one of the study tables started to laugh.

"And I don't intend to be."

"That's fine," he said, trying to keep his voice low. "I mean that's what I like about you. Well, sort of."

She left the library, but not before turning to him one last time as she was going out the door. "Think about it," she said, without any sign of anger in her voice.

He moved to the chair she'd been sitting in and leaned forward in the cubicle to get away from any looks that might be coming his way. He sat there, feeling thoroughly mixed up by what had just happened. He tried to straighten out in his mind where it had turned sour. In the end he gave up on it, stood up from the seat, and took off to the weight room, figuring that maybe there he could work off some of his frustration.

In his bedroom a few nights later he discovered that there had been at least one Beothuk living on an island not far from Marten in the early 1800s. It said in one of the books he had checked out from the library that on Red Ochre Island archeologists had uncovered parts of a Beothuk skeleton. It was the same island where his grandfather and his family had once lived. Perhaps that was where the pendant had come from.

It sounded like it could be a good start to his assignment. There was so much information in the books and magazine articles he had found in the library that he was starting to wonder if he'd ever be able to make sense of it all and fit it into ten pages. Now he was figuring that he could begin the paper by talking about the discovery and then work back in time and tell what the way of life of the dead person must have been like.

He wondered if Nancy knew about the skeleton. Maybe he would make it a point to ask her? Since their meeting in the library a few days before, he'd been staying away from her. It was like there was a fence or something between them, and just no way of getting through to her. In fact he knew that, if he was honest, he'd have to admit she didn't really seem to care that he was desperate to get to know her better. What had she done to make him feel wanted around her, except look at him the way she did with those eyes?

For a while he was thinking that maybe he should just forget about playing up to her again. He had actually tried it, for a day or so. But then she was back on his mind as much as ever. Why couldn't he get rid of the feeling that he just had to get her to like him?

She wasn't particularly good-looking, not in the way that some of the girls in the school were. In fact she was average in most of the ways fellows usually thought about girls. But there was something special about her. To him there was, at least. Although he seemed to be the only person in the school to think it. Nobody else paid her much attention, except to laugh at the old fur coat she often wore to school. It looked like muskrat and like it once belonged to her grandmother or something. David thought it was kind of neat, stylish in an offbeat way.

She seemed happy enough that people left her alone, although he had no way of knowing for sure. It bothered him.

He was thinking that next week he'd have a chance to find out. On Thursday their class was taking a trip into St. John's. Every year's grade ten class went there for a tour of the university and colleges, to get them thinking about what they would do once they finished with high school.

Ever since the school year started in September the class had been planning for it. They'd held car washes and bake sales and teenage dances and sold tickets on a ten-speed bike, all to raise money for the trip. They had discussed and argued over what other places they would go once they got there. It was two days off from regular school, and if it turned out anything like the trips that classes in other years had taken, they would be making the most of every minute of it.

He figured that traveling a hundred and fifty miles on a bus with her and back again, there were bound to be lots of chances to get to know her better. He'd be able to talk to her without anyone thinking much of it. And maybe, with so much going on, she just might loosen up a bit. For sure she wasn't going to be as serious as she looked most of the time.

That was one side of the trip to St. John's. There was another side, too, that was just as much on his mind. He knew from his mother that St. John's was where his real father was living. The opportunity was there to visit him if he made up his mind that was what he wanted to do. Sometimes he wished he'd never thought of it. In lots of ways it would be easier not to have to make the decision, but now it was there to be made and he would have to do something about it.

He wanted to see him, yet he was scared to. He didn't want his mother thinking that he might be scared and he certainly didn't want that message to get back to the old man.

When he first mentioned to her that he was thinking about going to see him, she had dismissed the idea. He figured she was hoping that it would just pass out of his mind. But a few days later, when he was moping around the house more than usual, she came in his room and wanted to know if that was the reason he was so down in the mouth.

"Do you really think you should?" she asked. "He might be nothing like you expect."

"What do you think I expect?"

"I'm not sure. I told you I didn't like him enough to marry him."

"That shouldn't stop me."

"Nothing is going to stop you if you really make up your mind to do it. I'm just saying you better be prepared to live with whatever you find."

"You just don't want me to do it, that's all."

"At first I didn't. Now I'm not sure. Maybe it would be the best thing."

That wasn't what he expected. Now there seemed to be some pressure on him to make up his mind to do it. He didn't want it to look like it was anyone's decision but his own.

"I made up my mind long ago. I'm going to see him. All I want you to do is let him know I'm coming."

"You're sure?"

"Sure, I'm sure."

She stood up to leave. "Maybe he'll be really glad to see you, you never know," she said.

"Just maybe he will."

She went out and closed the door behind her. Now at least he had it settled, he thought. He wasn't sure if it made him feel any better.

He stayed in his room a long time after that. He could hear the sounds of TV programs coming from the living room, programs that he never missed when he was in the house. Eventually a knock came on his door.

"Yeah?" he said, quickly opening up one of the schoolbooks that lay next to him on the bed.

"Can I come in?" It was the old man. He hadn't been in his room in weeks, and whenever he had come in before he had always done it without knocking.

David sat up straighter on the bed. "Sure."

The old man opened the door and looked in. "Is something wrong?"

"No. Should there be?" David said.

"Just askin'. Thought you must be sick or something."

"I'm doing my homework."

"Okay."

David could sense that he had something he wanted to say. Whatever it was David didn't want to hear it.

"I got a test tomorrow. I got two chapters that I haven't looked at yet."

"Okay." He stood there, still looking at him. Hardly moving.

"Ask Mom if she'd make me a snack."

"Sure."

He left then. After a few minutes David got up and went out in the kitchen to head off any chance that the old man might bring back the snack himself.

Dauoodaset

When I return to our camp today it is with the two killings tied to my back. The sun is still shining strong. It is hard to hide my pleasure. There has not been fresh meat in our camp for many days. My father greets me with much smiling and even my mother loses her face of sorrow.

It is time for happiness among us. My kill is small, but it is a sign of good things for my people. We make much of a little when it is all we have. My mother talks of a meal with the circle of families, when we will eat as one.

She makes a soup of the partridge, letting it boil a long time so that its goodness will fill the pot. Tonight we eat under the sky. There is no wind and a big moon lights up the night, signs of the good favor shown now to us.

Edeshnon, the leader of our mamateek band, drinks from the soup pot first. Drink is given then to the youngest of us, Shamoonon. They are the two guidemarks of our families. One leads us to a new life for our people. The other is the sign of our people's life yet to come.

I drink from the pot in turn according to my age. Baethasuit will not drink from the family pot because of her cough. Soup is poured into a small vessel and carried inside the mamateek to her resting pit. The passing of the pot goes on until all have drunk from it a second time. Now the flesh of the bird and its bones are divided among our circle. Waumaduit takes great care to be sure that each part is given in fairness.

Now, she says to my father, it is good that I have made so many new eating vessels. They smile together.

The drink warms my body, spreading its goodness through all of it and making strength where there was hunger before. I keep the meat in my mouth a long time before I swallow. The taste of fresh meat brings memories painful in their distance. I suck at the larger bone from my bowl. The smaller one is brittle. Its pieces lie sharp in my mouth. I spit them out, like I do the wanting to swallow them.

The marten too is cooked now in a soup pot. For seven people it is too small to roast over the fire. I long for meat rough against my teeth, meat to tear and chew like the fall caribou. These thoughts will go away in time. Let us be thankful for what we have now to eat.

After the food is all gone and Waumaduit has collected the bones for the bonesack, I sit in my resting pit as I like to do and think of my tomorrow's work.

Cosheewet begins a song. It startles me, for there have been no songs around our fires for many days. It is a new song, or an old one whose words I have not heard before. He sings of the cold days before the breakup of the ice in spring, hard days for our people. He sings of the days ahead when we will be tested more.

And then it is of me that he sings, how I brought fresh meat when there was great need. It is a hunter-thanking song. My first one. I look away shyly. They are made only when the times of which they speak must be remembered for our children. Many men do not have their first thanking song until they are much older. My father has four, which he has taught to me. Now I have one.

Cosheewet sings it over and over. He knows I am holding the words to my memory. The others look on me. My father knows the pride I feel and I know the pride of my father and my mother. Waumaduit looks at me and a small smile shows on her face. I think of the days when she had much to be happy about.

The others have joined with Cosheewet in the singing. Their voices fill our mamateek and I must stand to receive their praise. At the end of the singing the others shout their cheers. I sit down, very happy that I hunt now equal with any man and better than some. For I have now a great hunter-thanking song to pass to my children.

All the smiling makes good feelings in our mamateek tonight. It is my uncle the singer who thinks now that we should play at the dicing game. I am eager to play. I feel the spirits still with me and they will help me win.

The four of us men sit in a circle with three arrows each by our sides. Cosheewet opens his pouch of gaming pieces. He has the pieces we most like to play with. They have been made with great care from caribou antler, each piece carved on one side and with much marking, stained with ochre to show it well. We will play fives. Cosheewet chooses the best five pieces and spreads them before our circle. He looks at each of us. Each in turn raises a hand to show they are good. He drops them in the gaming bowl.

Now we must see who will be the first to challenge. My uncle shakes the pieces in the bowl and tosses them in the air. They land on our playing ground. Three of the pieces land showing their marks, two their flats. Cosheewet has scored three. Edeshnon tosses. He scores only one. My father, shaking the bowl with much noise and laughing, tosses high in the air. On the landing, all five show their mark side. Father shouts for his good fortune and passes the bowl to me. I collect up the pieces and make my toss. Three markers is all.

Now the play begins. Father chooses to challenge Cosheewet. He places one arrow before him and my uncle does the same. They toss in turn. Father makes four, my uncle two, and he wins Cosheewet's arrow. He turns to Edeshnon. Again he wins. This time it is three markers for father and two for Edeshnon.

Now he must challenge me. I feel the spirits with me and I am eager to begin. I lay not one, but two of my arrows before me. He is surprised, but gives a smile. Quickly he puts another from his pile out in front. I roll the pieces over each other many times in the bowl and toss them sharply to the playing ground. A two. It is not good. Father is pleased by my bad toss and throws now with sureness to win. But it is a blanker that he throws. Five flats, not one mark! His shouting is cut to silence. It is a double win for me. My father, I laugh, you are wounded like the marten I arrowed.

Now it is me to challenge. I choose Cosheewet and win again. Then Edeshnon, but my good fortune leaves me and Edeshnon wins. Still I have five arrows.

The playing goes on for a long while. My mother and my cousin have gathered around us. My mother works with her sewing, but her eyes are with the game we play. The two of them groan each time a pile falls to one arrow. They make loud talk among themselves over who will win.

Cosheewet is the first to fall out. He loses his last arrow to Father. Then, after much near falling out, it is Father to go. I win his last arrow and add it to my pile. I have eight, Edeshnon four.

Sometimes it is our way to stop at this, to have two to win and two to lose. But I want to win Edeshnon's four and make a one-man win. Edeshnon is our leader and perhaps this is not the way for me who has just been given a hunter-thanking song. Father looks at me with a worried face. I do not look at my mother.

I put four of my arrows before me and begin to roll the gaming pieces in the bowl. Edeshnon shows no bad feelings.

"Dauoodaset," he says, "you are still on the hunt. I am no marten. I am the partridge that got away." He puts all his arrows before him.

I smile at him while I roll the pieces. I make a loud cry like my father and toss them hard. They strike the ground. Three marks, two flats.

"Spirits smile at you, Dauoodaset," he says, knowing I wished for better.

Edeshnon makes much of his toss, talking like one who has won many times before. He snaps his wrist and the pieces spread wide across the ground. Two. Only two marks show.

He hands me quickly his pile of arrows. "Here," he says, "make good with these. More arrows, more kills. Our people have faith in you."

It is not said with kindness in his voice. The arrows he gives me are marked as if they must make kills. He expects me to prove again that I can bring food to our people. The words he spoke feel heavy on my mind.

I take the arrows and go back to my resting pit. My mother looks on me with anger and with pity. I do not want either of her looks. I am a man of my own thinking and I will do what is right for me.

As the fire burns low in our mamateek and the others are asleep in their resting pits, I lie awake thinking of the day that has passed, a day of many different stirrings in my spirit.

We have gone through bad times when many of our people have died from the cough and from attacks made with guns by the whiteman. I have seen hard times that took us away from all of our families together at the great lake and made us come in search of new land where no whitedevil's foot has walked. I will fight to keep my people safe. I will use my arrows well. They will protect my people and keep the hunger killers away from them.

David

The bus left for St. John's at eight forty-five on Thursday morning. As it pulled away from the school grounds a wild cheer rang through it. After the months of looking forward to the trip, they were finally on their way.

By the time the bus reached the highway the excitement had died down to a buzz of conversation, broken now and then by laughter and muffled squeals. Almost everyone had settled into some section of seats with a group of friends. A few sat by themselves, lost in the rock and roll driving through the headphones of their Walkmans.

Only Nancy looked to be really alone. David could see that she was dividing her time between the paperback she had in her hand and the scenery outside. He had been sitting with Jim and two girls for a while, but he moved away from them and settled down with his Walkman a few seats behind her. From there he kept a close watch on what she was doing, trying not to be obvious about it.

He had made up his mind that during the trip he was going to work it so that she would have to deal with him. Make or break the relationship. The only question was the timing. He waited in the seat for ten minutes, and then almost moved, but then thought it might be better to wait a while longer.

Finally, after a couple more songs, he moved up the aisle and asked the bus driver how long he thought it would take to get there. On the way back he stopped and slid into the empty seat in front of her.

"Hi, what are you reading?"

"Nothing," she said and put the book away before he had a chance to see the cover.

"Top secret, is it?"

"Private."

"Sorry."

"I'll make a deal with you," she said bluntly. "You keep your secrets and I'll keep mine."

"You got it." He was determined not to let anything she said get to him.

What he realized was that she wasn't really talking like she was mad at him. She was being blunt, and perhaps no more than that. Maybe she wasn't really mad those other times — maybe it was just her normal way of talking to people.

"Know something?" he said after a while of fiddling with the Walkman.

"What?"

"I think we could like each other if you'd give it a chance." He imagined what would have happened if he had said that to any of the other girls he knew.

She didn't laugh. She didn't even smile. She looked, in fact, like she almost expected it. "Do you really think so?"

"Try it."

"Who said I haven't already?" she said.

"Come off it. I'm not that weird. Let's face it, you're afraid to get to know me, afraid you'll find out you like me."

He couldn't believe he was really saying that. He knew it was what he had been thinking, but couldn't believe he was being that bold.

"I like you," she said.

"You got a funny way of showing it."

"I keep things to myself."

"What good is that to me?"

She grinned at him. It was the first time he had seen her do that without its looking like it was planned. A definite crack in that shell of hers, he was thinking.

"And you don't have to be so serious all the time," he said. "Loosen up a little."

There was a laugh. It had a serious edge to it, though, that left David wondering if he'd gone a bit too far.

"Maybe I'm wrong," he said quickly, "but I just think it would be easier for you that way."

"I'm happy the way I am."

"You don't look very happy."

"The way I look has got nothing to do with it."

"Okay, okay." Then he said, more for himself than for what good he thought it would do, "I don't know why I'm at this. I'd be better off leaving you alone."

"No, you wouldn't."

"Where's it getting me?"

"You'll find out."

He shook his head. "What's that supposed to mean?"

She stared at him. "Let's keep one thing straight," she said.

"Anything, anything."

"Don't think you can change me. Take me for what I am. And for now we'll be friends."

It was a while before he said anything. "I guess, if that's what you want." He shrugged.

He put the headphones on so he wouldn't be expected to say anything more. Perhaps that was the only way to make something work between them — give up trying to understand her, forget her bluntness, and believe that she really did like him.

Still, there was a lot missing if it was going to be any more than a friendship. Each time he glanced out at her through the music filling his head, he knew he wanted it to be more.

If Nancy had been the only thing on his mind during the bus ride he might have taken it a bit further. When she mentioned secrets, he was thinking there was a lot about himself that he wouldn't be willing to share. A bit later Dalton, one of the two teachers who were with them on the bus, came up to him and said, "I had a call from your mother last night. That's fine with me. Just let me know before you go." That got him thinking about it even more.

What to call him when they did meet face-to-face? It seemed stupid in a way for him to be spending so much time wondering about that. He'd only ever thought of him as his "real father," never really had any reason to use a name. He was hoping there would be no need to use one now, when they did meet.

There were more important things to think about. Did he really want to see him? What would he say to him when he did?

But even as he was riding in the taxi to the house that night it was on his mind what to call him. That first look between them — did he have the right house, is he the one?

The taxi reached the street quicker than he thought it would. They passed 52. The other side of the street, but it couldn't be far. Number 25. He asked the taxi driver to stop before they reached it. He wanted time to walk up to it.

It was an old row house, joined to the many others like it on the street, each one painted a different color. Number 25 was a dark shade of green, not a color he thought anyone would paint a house, but not shabby. It was no worse than any of the others.

It was just a few feet from the sidewalk to the concrete steps that led to the front door. He looked up and saw a girl a few years younger than himself looking down at him through a picture window. He couldn't just stand there. He'd have to walk up the steps and knock.

A man answered. He was big, much bigger than David had expected. He was buttoning up a white shirt over a big gut. He looked like he'd just woken up from a nap.

"Hello," David said. When he looked closely at the man's face David knew it had to be him. He could see now where the odd blue color of his own eyes had come from.

"David?" he said. "You gotta be David."

He nodded.

The man held out a thick hand, like something swollen. "John," he said.

"Hi." David tried as best he could to make it feel as if his hand had some strength to it.

"Your mother said you'd be coming." He stood back from the doorway. "Come in, come in."

David squeezed past him. He stooped down to untie his sneakers.

"Never mind about that. A little bit o' dirt never hurt nothin'," he said, laughing.

David thought of saying it was no trouble, but he decided it wasn't worth it. He straightened up again.

He followed him into the living room. The girl he had seen through the window was sitting at the end of a couch near the TV set, one leg curled under her. She wore long, dangling earrings that caught the light when she moved. On the TV screen people were jumping up and down and there was a car with lights flashing numbers behind it.

"My God, Gloria, turn that thing down. It's a wonder we're not all deaf," the man said.

She turned it down, but it was still loud.

"This here's David. Remember I told you someone might be coming."

"Hi," she said, glancing at him. "Dad, I told ya that blond one was gonna win. Lucky, wha'? I wouldn't mind being her."

"Hi," David said. She smiled at him.

He smiled back. He turned behind him, in the direction of a woman coming down from upstairs.

"And this is Margaret. Marg, my dear, here he is."

Her lips were a deep red color and she smelled of perfume. Her hair was long and straight, and tied back tight behind her neck.

"Hello," she said quietly and smiled. She was overweight, too, and it seemed odd to David that her voice wasn't louder.

"Well," her husband said quickly, "we might as well sit down, right? No use standing when we could be sitting, right?"

David sat on the end of the couch opposite Gloria, and the man offered him something to drink. "Gloria, my love, go get us something from the fridge."

She didn't say anything, but he could see she wasn't too happy about having to miss some of the TV program. She took her dead slow time.

"I'll do it," her mother said, irritated with how long it was taking Gloria to get up off the couch. She stood up and left the room.

"Marg," the man called out after her, laughing, "he's too

young for a beer." David smiled at him, knowing it would make things easier if he did.

"So," he said while they waited for his wife to get back, "you're on some kinda school trip, are ya?"

"Yeah."

"Came in by bus, right?"

"Yeah. Got in here about one thirty."

"Good trip?"

"Yeah."

There was quiet for a while. "And what are you now, David? Fourteen?"

"Fifteen."

"Right."

He took out a pack of cigarettes from his shirt pocket and lit one. "Guess you don't smoke?"

David shook his head.

"Got too many brains for that. What about a girlfriend? Got a girlfriend, I bet."

Gloria looked over at him. He grinned but didn't answer.

When the woman came back and handed him a glass of what tasted like Diet Coke, it was easier. She had given her husband a beer and he started talking about all the different shapes of bottles that beer came in now and what a bugger of a time it was when he brought back the empties, especially when there was a crowd over and they were all drinking different brands. He still drank the same brand that he always did, though — Dominion. David was thinking that it was the same brand that the old man back home bought, and how that was a bit strange.

He talked about beer and then he talked about how much he liked sports on TV. Except football. He never could understand the game. Never really wanted to understand it because he never did like it in the first place.

Golf he could watch all day. Funny thing. Never set foot on a golf course in his life, but he'd never miss it on TV.

David said he liked tennis. Yeah, the man said, tennis too he got a kick out of sometimes. Especially that McEnroe. He liked it when he got savage with the ref.

His wife had gone into the kitchen again and Gloria was watching her TV program, and listening to what they were saying at the same time.

"Dad."

A young fellow, who looked to David to be about the same age as Brad, came rushing through the front door and into the living room. "Dad, I gotta have some money to go to the arena — two bucks."

"Where's what I gave you last night?"

"Spent."

"I got five bucks to last me till the check comes. I can't give you what I haven't got."

The fellow looked at David. "You growin' a moustache?" he said.

David put his fingers to his face and grinned awkwardly.

"Christ, Johnny, don't be so brazen," his father said. "Your mother's in the kitchen. Go see if she got any money to give ya."

"Don't mind him," he said to David when the young fellow had left.

David took another swallow of Diet Coke and the man drank some more of his beer. Gloria turned her attention back to the TV.

"What grade you in now?"

Before he had a chance to answer, a loud bang, like a chair falling over, could be heard coming from the kitchen.

"So what!" Then the slam of an outside door.

"He's a hard case," the man said, shaking his head and

huffing a laugh through his nose. "It's the crowd he hangs around with."

"I'm in grade ten," David said. "Two more years to go before I graduate."

His wife came in with a mug and the spoon still in it, and sat down between him and Gloria.

David was starting to feel warm. Even though he had his coat unzippered, he didn't want to take it off without being asked.

"John," she said, "I'm sure I'm coming down with the flu again."

David could feel the weight of her close to him. She was a lot heavier than his mother. Grayer, too, although he knew his mother dyed her hair. David could smell smoke from her clothes. His mother was death on smoking.

"Don't mind the mess," she said. "We knew you'd be coming, but we didn't know when."

He wouldn't have called it messy. For what they had, it was tidy enough. The picture of the Pope on the wall across from him was crooked. That was about all.

"Have some more," the man said. "Gloria, go get David here some more drink."

"No, thanks."

"You're sure? There's more out there. You're sure, now?"

"No, that's okay."

"If he don't want it, he don't want it."

"Gloria, love, go get your father another beer," he said.

She grunted and got up slowly to go to the kitchen. "Who was your slave before you had me?" she said as she passed him.

"So," he said to David, "what's new in Marten? I worked there when they put the pavement through. God, that seems like a hell of a long time ago now."

"Not much, I guess."

"Old Silas Gillingham still on the go? That fellow used to run off some wicked shine, I can tell ya."

"He's dead now."

"That right? Yes, I guess he would be. He musta been close on seventy when I knew him and I guess that's twenty years ago now."

David let that pass.

"And your mother is fine, is she?"

He nodded.

"And your father?"

He nodded again.

"He worked on building the road the same time I did. He was a hard-working man. And tough." He laughed to himself, like it was a private joke.

Nobody said anything for a while. David was uncomfortable, but he tried hard not to let it show. He wanted him to be the one to feel like he had to say something. Then Gloria came back in the room with his beer.

"We was hoping you woulda come for supper," the man said. "We put on extra thinkin' maybe you might turn up."

"Oh, shit!" Gloria yelled. "She screwed it up. Now she's lost it all."

"Who?"

"If I was her I woulda stopped at five thousand."

Now they all had their eyes on the TV. "Turn it up a bit," her mother said, leaning forward.

David looked at it too, even though he couldn't have cared less about what it was. He was thinking about other things he wanted to talk about. He couldn't see any way of bringing them up. Or any point in it, probably.

"Guess I should be going now," he said after a while. He stood up and started zippering up his coat.

"Lots o' time, lots o' time," the man said. "We was only just startin' to get to know each other."

"I told the teacher I wouldn't be gone long."

"You don't have to go yet?"

"I should, really."

"You're sure, now?"

"I think I better."

"Now you know where we live, right? You'll have to come back some other time."

"Thanks."

He said good-bye and was out the front door and down over the steps without a handshake. They had squeezed in something about saying hello to his parents for them. He held up his hand — good-bye again, and promised that he would.

Walking up the street, he was sorry he said that he would. He hoped they knew how relieved he was to be out of the house. He wished he hadn't tried to cover it all up.

He couldn't really decide what he thought of him. He just knew it wasn't that good.

Dauoodaset

It has been many days since my kills, and the meat pile in our storehouse is falling low. I have gone again in search of food, but have returned each time with only a few berries dug from beneath the snow. The cold has returned as bitter as before. The river ice that for two days was skimmed with water now is frozen thick again. My people stare with eyes that are weak with weariness, narrow and with little hope. I cannot share their gloom. I cannot let myself sink into it. I feel apart.

This cold will pass and we will find our way to the saltwater. I am making ready a place to build a new canoe. It will be the one to lead us to a new life for our people.

When I tell Edeshnon this he has no words to encourage me. He speaks only of wasted arrows. He does not even talk long on that. His own hunting has brought no meat to us.

I have no one to share my hopes, only Shamoonon, the young one. He comes to watch me. He sits weakly about and stares at every move. He is thinking if there will be a time when he will need to know such a thing.

My father taught me when I was of that age, but now my

father does not come to where I work. He tells me I should save my strength for other things. Our old canoes will be good enough, he says, and it is still cold, not the time to build. If our ways are false the spirits will not show us pity.

It is not so. Not one of the old canoes is as strong as it must be for our journey. And it is not pity we need. We must do all we can for ourselves. I too mourn for the days when our people were many living together, with food and comfort for all. Again we will live together and have days of plenty. It must be our way to look ahead.

If there was another in our camp of my age we would have strength together to go farther from our mamateek in search of food. I miss Keeushuwit. He shared the good times of our young days. We grew to be men together.

Keeushuwit went away and did not return. He left the camp of our people in anger to take the nets the whitemen used to rob us of our salmon. We did not see him again.

Keeushuwit was a trickster. Once we laid sappy cones of the spruce tree between the furs of his cousin's resting pit on his marriage night. We bent with laughter many times over our secret. He would make noises during our night ceremonies and pretend he was not the one. He always would smile and make fun even in the hardest times. The last days we were together we made a promise that soon we would go and make a hunting journey of many days. I do not want to think of that now.

Our canoes are built of spruce wood and the bark of birch trees. They rise high at the ends and in the middle, so they are quick to move about and not take aboard the waves in rough water. They are of little weight, easy to carry over land between the waterways.

My first job is to cut bark from the biggest of the birch trees. It is not easy, for the frost has made the bark more brittle than in summer. I choose a day when the sun shines long on the trees. I begin my work carefully with my best knife and a rock pounder. I cut the longest strips I can to make less the work of sewing them together. I have lashed together tree limbs to make a climber so I can reach the tall parts of the trees. My cuts are not deep. It is not our way to strip bare and kill the trees. A canoe would not be safe to journey in if it was made from the bark of such a tree.

Shamoonon is near at my feet and I show him the way. If he had the strength I would give him the tools to try his hands at the work. But he talks with eagerness in his questions. Someday, I tell him, we will make together a canoe just for his hunting. He smiles, for the first time since he has been with me. It brings thoughts of Keeushuwit to me.

"Shamoonon," I say to him, "you will need a canoe to paddle with the young girls. When we camp again with our people you will win the smiles of young Konaubee with your skill in the canoe."

It brings laughter to him. "I have no fondness for her."

"Who is it, then?" He smiles. "Young Shamoonon, you do dream of her I think."

"No."

"You talk with her in your dreams."

"Crazy."

"Holding her like a married one."

"Like you dream of Shanawdithit."

We laugh together.

"I know," he says. "I saw it when you were together. Making love for each other with your eyes."

Now it is I who turn the color that ochre has to hide. "You make me lose my place on the tree," I say, making as if I am angry. "I cannot do my work well when you make such fun."

"It was you who started, Dauoodaset. Your tongue stings your own mouth."

"Here, steady the climber. You want me to fall?"

Shamoonon becomes my companion, my steady helper. When I begin to strip away the bark he holds apart the lower parts as I work my way up the tree. We sing the old songs that I remember from the work times when we lived by the great lake. Soon the long sheets of bark lie curled on top of the ground.

But our work has to stop. My father calls from a distance to help with a vapor bath for Baethasuit, my sick aunt. She is worse now. The vapor baths help her only a little.

My uncle has cleared away the ashes from the fire rocks and has filled a bark vessel with water for pouring. A frame of spruce is over the hot rocks and over it is a covering of bark.

Baethasuit is too weak to walk and two of us must carry her to the place. We sit her inside on a bed of boughs and wrap her warmly with furs. My mother sits with her and pours water over the hot rocks to make the steam. Wisps of steam drift out into the cold air. My father seals the door tighter. Hard coughing and spitting sounds cut into the silence like sharp pains into all of us. My mother crawls out and closes back the door. We sit together and call to the spirits to help her.

When it is too much for her, we carry her back to the mamateek. I am thinking it may be for the last time. Her head falls against my uncle and she is too weak to bring it up again. We lay her back in her resting pit and when I look at her I remember the dying of my grandmother.

"Can I help?"

He took a while to answer. "Remember what we said about secrets."

This time he was the odd one out. She had been the one to start things between them. But still they weren't fitting together right.

He looked at her. If he could have known he'd feel comfortable doing it, he would have just stared and stared. The red light seemed to bring a peacefulness to her face that he had not seen before. There was a look in her eyes that made him want to touch her. He could feel himself stir.

It didn't seem to bother her the way he kept having to stare and look away and stare again. He lost the need to say anything. And, without thinking about what she might think, he moved closer and kissed her gently on the mouth. At first only their lips were touching, but when he felt a hint of her lips pressing against his, he put his arms around her and held her tightly.

For a moment it was wonderful. Then he felt her wanting him to let her go. He did it as gently as he could. He grinned quietly, wanting to appear shyer than he had been.

She met his look with a brief glance. A touch of regret? He couldn't tell. She didn't say anything. When she turned and walked away it was deliberately slow, as if she didn't want to offend him. Then she started to run. He wasn't sure what it meant.

But he was glad he had done it. He was thinking it was the most positive thing he had done all day. He stayed under the exit light for a while longer, and when he went back he had the feeling that he could be more like his usual self.

They were all late getting to bed that night. The next day

the teachers had them up at eight. By nine thirty they were dragging themselves through a tour of the university. It was noon before their energy levels returned to normal. Late in the afternoon, after a couple of hours at the Avalon Mall, the bus took them to the Newfoundland Museum — the last stop before heading back to Marten.

Nancy was the first one off the bus. She hadn't said much to him during the day, but what she had said was pleasant enough. David figured that, if anything, the meeting the night before had improved their relationship. He was so sure of it that as they were entering the building he ran and caught up with her and suggested they walk through the exhibits together. She agreed.

They all stopped in front of the information desk. The guy behind the desk stood up and said a few words about the museum. He explained the best route to take in going through it. Then he directed them up a flight of stairs.

At the top of the stairs was a large showcase. Inside it a great horned owl, wings spread wide, hovered over a snowshoe hare. David was fascinated at how lifelike they were.

"Great detail."

Nancy nodded, but then she added, "A waste, don't you think?"

He was about to ask her what she meant, but she had already gone inside the main exhibition room. He walked around to the other side of the case to get a look at it from a different angle.

He jumped back. A sharp, whimpering moan, like something from a frightened animal, came at him from inside the room.

He turned quickly to go inside. But just as he did, Nancy came rushing past him, a hand over her mouth, her eyes full of terror. She pushed her way back down the stairs, past the crowd of students on their way up.

For a second David stood frozen, not sure what to do. He took a quick look inside where Nancy had been, but he could see nothing that he didn't expect to see — display cases of Beothuk artifacts, a reconstruction of what looked like a burial site.

He raced back down the stairs. At the main entrance he met Dalton.

"She ran outside," he said, "like she'd seen a ghost or something. You go one way and I'll go the other."

He walked as fast as he could down the street, looking between the buildings, desperate to catch a glimpse of her. She was nowhere to be found. He started to yell out her name, but then he stopped, thinking it might frighten her off. He kept going until he saw a traffic cop just up the street ahead of him. He retraced his steps, taking a closer look down the alleyways he had looked into before.

Suddenly, down one, he saw a flash of black — maybe the coat she'd been wearing? He ran down between the buildings.

It was Nancy. She was standing with her back to him, her head and shoulder leaning against a dirty brick wall. She was making a low, unbroken moan, almost a chant.

He walked around her and looked into her face. It was wet with tears. Her eyes were closed. She seemed not to know where she was or that there was anyone near her.

"Nancy," he said to her quietly, "what's the matter?"

She didn't answer.

"Are you all right?"

Her eyes opened slowly, then blinked heavily when she realized that someone was talking to her.

"What's wrong?"

"Nothing you can do," she said.

He moved closer. She moved away.

"Nothing you can do. Leave me alone."

"I want to help you." He reached out with both his hands and held her shoulders.

Anger swept across her face. "You're all alike!" she yelled. "Let go of me. You have no right!"

She ran off. She stopped a short distance away and leaned up against the building again.

He left her and went to look for Dalton. When he found him they ran back up the street together. Just before they reached the alleyway, Nancy emerged, her eyes red and swollen. She was trying to look normal.

"Are you okay?" Dalton asked her.

She acted as if nothing strange had happened. She insisted that she was fine, that it was just claustrophobia, something that had happened to her before.

She walked back to the bus with them. By that time all the other students were aboard, waiting. They stared at her as she walked to her seat. She tried to smile and said she was sorry if she had frightened anyone.

She sat down in the seat that had been hers since they started the trip. She made a pillow with her coat and closed her eyes. She hardly moved from that position all the way to Marten.

It wasn't long after she sat down that the noise of people talking again filled the bus. David sat by himself. He didn't want to have to answer their questions about what had happened. And he didn't want to hear their comments about what they thought of her now.

Dauoodaset

It is my work now to dig the roots that I will split into strips and use to sew the sheets of bark into one. In the past the splitting was the work of my mother, but I have not the boldness to ask her. It is enough that she is willing to show me the way. Even that she does with sharpness in her voice. I look with pity beyond her words to her frail fingers and the tired look in her face.

Shamoonon is there to clear the roots of dirt after I struggle to draw them from the earth. The ground is hard with frost and does not give way for my digging. My hands are sore from the scraping. When large rocks block my way, I feel heavy in my heart and think that this may be useless work. But I fight what I feel and try to think that the hardness is a test the spirits have laid before me. When my people see my stubbornness and see the work when it is done, it will make them have new hope for us.

Edeshnon has called me foolish. Not before me, but before my father, who he knew would tell me. My body inside went tight with anger.

I call him Old Man. He is not the leader that is best for our people. He mourns for his past, when times were different. He is leading us into sorrow for ourselves, not out of it. Already we should be making ready for the voyage to the saltwater. He sits and chants his words to the spirits as if it is our only hope. I know what it is I would do. But I am not of the age to speak. To his face the words I would say would not be heard. And the words I feel could not be said.

After many days I have gathered enough roots. But the work is only a little more easy. The rawness of my hands makes the splitting of the roots and the sewing together of the bark with the strips a painful job. Shamoonon is of great help. He warms the roots near a fire to draw the frost from them and make them bend. There is no singing in our work now, only a hard and quiet steadiness to finish what we have to do.

Upon the ground the sheets of bark together make a broad skin for the canoe. The sides are weighted down with rock to stop their curling. We rest and look at what we have done. Shamoonon says it is good. But his thin face looks pitiful with worry, not the way for a soon-to-be man. I do what I can to keep his thoughts on the reason for our task.

"Shamoonon, do you know what lies where this river ends?"

"The great sea."

"And more."

"Fishes, mussels, seals thick with fat and meat. Food for all our people and places to live in peace."

"No whiteman?"

"The stories of that place tell of no whiteman."

"These stories are old."

"Old, but true. We have traveled far away from them."

"It will be a great day when we reach that place."

When we start once more at our task it is again with song, softer than for the cutting of the bark, but stronger in our hearts. We can see now an end to our work.

The days are warming again. Only a scattering of snow lies about our camp. Only in the deepest woods does the snow lie heavy. All across the river, the ice is changing to water. Soon what is left of the ice will break apart and there will be open water to the sea.

Long spruce pieces, three lengths of my body, we curve and lash together at the ends with split roots to make the frame for the canoe. It must hold together well. It will have much more than the weight of my body to bear. It must bear the hopes of all our people.

We are busy pounding stakes into the ground to hold steady the frame for the work of covering it with the bark, when the sharpened voice of Edeshnon calls us through the trees.

"Dauoodaset. Shamoonon. Come away. Stop your needless work. Baethasuit has been taken from us. We must prepare for her burial. What strength you have not wasted is needed now. Bring your bark for her burial sack."

My heart quickens. It is what I knew would happen soon. Baethasuit has grown weaker and weaker each day. We follow my uncle and in our hands we carry the sheet of bark we have worked so hard to make. I cannot question Edeshnon at such a time as this. I think of Baethasuit and those who mourn for her, and wish in secret that her death had waited until after my canoe had its covering. We have buried our dead before without a sack of bark.

I cannot weep for Baethasuit. Her body lies at rest upon the earth, relieved that the coughing pain torments it no more. Her face is sunken skin drawn sharp across bone and is peaceful like a flower withered with frost is peaceful. She will find no misery where she goes.

A piece of bark, the length of her body, is cut from my

sheet and her body is laid on one side of it. Red ochre is spread thick over her flesh. Then she is dressed in a skin robe that is now too big for her body. My mother lays a string of bone pieces across her chest to protect her in her journey. Small cooking vessels are placed by her side. There are only dried out bones to put in them. Cosheewet lays long feathers about her to speed her journey.

The bark is folded over her body and sewn together with the strips of caribou hide that mother cuts from a snowshoe. The body is laid across a carrier made of poles. All of us who have the strength carry her to the place near the river where the land is high. It is the place Cosheewet has chosen for her grave.

The burial sack is placed upon the frosted ground, no earth is dug away. We stand and sing the passing songs. Edeshnon lifts his staff and speaks above our singing, calling the spirits to receive her, to join the many who have gone before.

When there are no words left to sing, it is the time when the sack is covered with rocks. What can be found nearby are gathered and placed gently upon the sack. The others of my people go back to the mamateek fire, and I am left with Shamoonon to search for more and bring them to the grave. I struggle with the weight of rocks harder than I have struggled to dig for roots. When darkness comes the burial sack is covered, not the rounded covering of the many graves we left at the great lake, but enough that the animals will be kept away and her journey can be made in peace.

This night my people sit in silence in the mamateek. They do not grieve her passing from them. Their grief is for themselves. Her death is a sign of more death, they say.

I cannot stay among them. I go out into the night, even though it is cold. My hands pain with cuts from the piling of the rocks.

I sit and wonder at the night. Many times as a boy with

my father I would ask him questions of the stars and the changing moon. There was much he could not answer and there is much now for me still to wonder. Baethasuit has died. My people say she has gone to be with the others who have died. Where is she gone? Among the stars? It is hard to believe all that my people say when there is nothing to help me believe, only the words of the old people.

I lie upon the ground staring at the stars like sparks of fire among the blackness. I lie with hunger and cold and pain in my body. Yet I think there will be a time when all this will pass. I have strength still to make it pass.

I think my people do not have such strength. When I return to the mamateek I see the weakness of death in their eyes and in their thoughts.

"Edeshnon," I say, "I will go soon to the saltwater. It is not far."

He looks at me with eyes that say this is not the time to talk so loud and so bold.

My words lie among my people. It stirs them out of their grieving. Where there was only despair before, now they look at each other with signs of hope. My father casts looks at Old Man that he cannot put aside. Edeshnon must know that he has no better way to save us. His own body has grown too weak to lead us out of this place, but he is too strong in his head to say this to our people.

My father has to say, "Edeshnon, do we have another way? Can we know that the spirits in their mercy will send animals of the woods to our reach? Do we have the strength to go in search of them?"

The others say yes to me. Edeshnon is the only one silent. He does not like others to think for him.

Finally, he speaks. "Then go, Dauoodaset. Do as you say. Find the saltwater. Save us from the starvation that you think is sure to come to us."

"Edeshnon!" my father says sharply. I have not heard

him speak my uncle's name so before. "You will die of your own bitterness. Dauoodaset is our hope. Why must you choose to make it harder for us all? My son will go as you say and we will pray for him in his journey."

Old Man is silent. He looks at me as if I am a child who should have nothing to say.

"Must he go alone?" my mother asks.

"I am not afraid," I tell her. "I have the strength. I am a boy no longer who needs the guidance of an older one."

From the dark wall of the mamateek a voice rises over us all. "I will go with Dauoodaset. The journey will be easier with two." It is Shamoonon.

Edeshnon is quick to say, "You are weak, Shamoonon. You have not the strength to paddle such a distance."

"I am not without some strength and we will find food along the way. My weight will balance the canoe." His voice is strong, eager.

I have to tell him no. I worry that the journey will be too long and too hard for him. The journey will be mine alone.

He asks again, saying he will be of good help to me.

"No!" It is the loud voice of Old Man. "If Dauoodaset goes, he will go alone."

There are no more words said this night.

The next day Shamoonon is by my side when I cut more bark and dig more roots to make the covering piece as it was before. I work with more speed than the first time. There is not the frost so deep as before and the thoughts of the journey are strong in my mind.

At last the ice has broken apart in the river. When the bark is bound to the frame and the canoe complete in all its parts, there will be open water enough to lead me on my way down the river. I long for that day with all that is in me.

David

It was after dark by the time the bus arrived back at the school in Marten. The parking lot was lined with vehicles waiting to pick up the students. David stepped off the bus and looked around for his mother. He was surprised and a bit uneasy when he saw that the only one sitting in the pickup was the old man.

The old man got out, stood by the truck, and waited for David to walk across the parking lot. He took the overnight bag from his hand and dropped it into the back of the truck.

"Where's Mom?"

"Home. I wasn't doing much. I figured I might as well drive over myself and pick you up."

They got aboard the pickup. David could see Nancy standing by the main door of the school. They hadn't said a word to each other all the way back. When he'd left the bus she was still in her seat, waiting, it seemed, for everyone else to get off. As he walked by he had asked if she had a way home, and without looking at him, she had nodded. He didn't know what he thought of her anymore.

The pickup started down the road toward home. "Good trip?" the old man asked.

"Yeah. It was a lot of fun."

"You look tired."

"Didn't get much sleep last night."

There was silence between them. David figured he'd let it ride. But then the old man started asking him more questions about the trip. David could see it leading up to something that he knew for sure he didn't want to talk about.

"It was Mom's idea, wasn't it, for you to come and pick me up?"

"And mine."

"I don't want to talk about it, so it's no good to ask."

The old man waited for a while.

"She told me you went to see him. I'm glad you did. So, what happened?"

"Nothin'."

"C'mon, don't give me that. I'm not that stupid."

"We talked. He invited me back again."

"You goin'?"

"Maybe."

"You don't sound very sure."

"Don't worry about it."

David could hear him swear under his breath.

"You're the one who started this," David said to him.

"Started what?" The old man held back.

David turned his head and looked out the window at the woods rushing past him. After a while it was making him dizzy. "Slow down."

"What the hell am I supposed to say?" the old man burst out. "You're old enough now . . ."

"Old enough for what?"

"Old enough to have better sense."

"God, not that again."

"Shut up, for Christ's sake!"

"We've never gotten along, why should we start now?"

The old man's face was red with frustration. He glanced

in the rearview mirror, then jammed on the brakes and pulled the pickup over to the shoulder of the road.

He looked across the seat. David, dreading what might come next, continued to stare out the window.

"Look at me, for Christ's sake."

David turned his head toward him, but wouldn't look him straight in the face.

"Just what do you want from me?" the old man said, his voice loaded with anger.

David was determined not to sound like it bothered him. "You know yourself you don't treat me like the others."

"Maybe it's 'cause you're not like them. You ever think o' that?" the old man shot back.

"And we both know there's good reason for that."

"We do, don't we. But I'm the one who married your mother, remember that. She coulda married that other guy. She had her choice. Maybe it's your mother you should be blamin', not me."

"Don't drag Mom into this."

"Don't be so goddamned thickheaded. She's into it, 'cause she's the one who had you. And she's the one who said yes when I asked her to get married."

David wanted to be saying something, but he didn't know what.

"And I'll tell you why I asked her. 'Cause we both knew we loved each other. And don't say I ever resented you, 'cause I never. We always got along as best we could. Until this come up."

"As best we could," David repeated, as much to have something to say as anything.

"Okay, so it haven't all been easy. But if you'd learn to give a little for a change, think of other people besides yourself... You might start with your mother."

"Sure, blame it all on me." David knew he could have snapped back with more. There were plenty of things churning in the back of his mind, some of them there for years, some things not even his mother knew about. A few, he'd admit, were not very important. Others sure as hell were, like the fact the old man liked Brad a lot more than he ever liked him.

He wouldn't say anything now. The old man would accuse him of sounding like a kid.

He felt like something trapped, with no chance of escape. But no way was he about to give in to him. He straightened up more and looked at the old man like he hadn't proven a thing. Then he turned and looked out the side window again.

The old man put the pickup in gear. He waited for a minute, looking at him, David knew, all that time. Then he turned to check the road behind him and drove away.

It had given David plenty more to think about.

Over the past few weeks he had come to think that he had figured out a way to deal with the old man. Keep away from him as much as he could. Talk to him only when he had to. He figured he'd learn to accept him like he would an uncle he didn't like. Now he was forced to rethink it all. The old man wanted them to settle their differences. He never thought it would come to that.

They said very little to each other the rest of the evening. Most of the time David spent in the kitchen with his mother, talking to her and to Brad and Sandra. They wanted to know all about his trip. He had brought back a small present for each of them, plus a box of chocolates for the whole family, so it wouldn't look like he had deliberately left out the old man.

After Brad and Sandra had gone to bed and the old man was in the living room watching the news on TV, David stayed at the kitchen table, eating toast and drinking tea with his mother.

"I can see why you didn't marry him." He said it like it had been what they were talking about all along.

It was a long time before she answered.

"I never really liked him much."

"I guess he's okay in his own way."

"What did he say?" she asked.

"Nothing much. Nothing that really matters."

"I'm glad you went."

"I thought I'd feel something more. Like he would really mean a lot to me."

"Maybe you had yourself built up too much."

"He *is* my father."

"In one way. Not the way that counts."

She had said it so easily, yet he wasn't sure he agreed with her.

"It's for you to settle in your own mind," she said. "I settled it in mine years ago."

"Don't you feel anything for him now?"

"No."

Her answer was quick and definite. It left him wondering if she wasn't just trying to force him into making up his mind the way she wanted him to.

He wouldn't say anything else. He wanted time on his own to think about it.

"Remember," she said, "you're the one who went to him. In all those years he never so much as sent you a birthday card."

He knew she was looking at him. He wouldn't look up. He started talking about something else that happened on the trip. And, a little later, he started to yawn and he got up from the table. He said he thought he'd better go to bed early and catch up on all the sleep he'd missed.

Dauoodaset

The canoe is complete. It lies in grass, not water. Brown grass, no sight of green among it yet.

Looking at the curve of its keel and its ends rising high and slender makes me think of the many canoes that have brought my people across the land, and me now to the beginning of my journey.

The light of the evening sun makes a long shadow of my work. The gunwales dip and peak, dip and peak, like frozen waves. It is a strong canoe, stronger now than the man who made it. But I have not lost hope for the journey. My fear now is for my people, for we have come to the last of the caribou.

My people lie in pairs or alone. Weaker, hungrier, careless in their body habits. On their faces hangs loose and wrinkled skin, and their sunken eyes are closed more than they are open. They do not speak except to moan the fate that has fallen on them. My father spends his time in company with my mother. Her old look of worry is worn to grief. When she looks at me it is as if a dark shadow covers her eyes.

It is hard to be with them. It is better that I do other things. I want to work at making tight every seam of my canoe. I want to make it the best that it can be for my journey. It may be the only chance there will be for my people.

I am anxious to be going. The river water near our camp is almost clear, but my father warns of morning ice, how its sharpness can cut apart a canoe.

I cannot wait too long. The days suck away at my strength too. I feel my own body tired and slowing fast. If I wait longer I will be too weak to paddle. I will go, I tell my people, on the next day that breaks with a clear strong sun.

I sit by my canoe at the edge of the river and think of all that I have to do in the days that are ahead. I dream of the celebration that there will be when I return with my canoe heavy with fish and game. It will be a great day for our people.

I dream too of the days after that when all of our people will be together. It is Shanawdithit that I think of most. How good it will be to be with her again. I will hold her close to me and I will not be shy to show my longing for her. The feelings I have are too strong for my body so weak. It is pain now that I feel.

David

For several days after they returned from the trip to St.
John's he had very little to do with Nancy. He didn't avoid
her, but neither did he make a point of talking to her. It
bothered him that she hadn't given him an explanation for
what had happened. If she wasn't going to be straight with
him, he said to himself, then maybe that should be the end
of things between them.

Of course, he couldn't keep from thinking about her. He
found himself doing that a lot, a lot more than he thought
he should. And when their eyes did meet by chance in the
classroom or in the corridors, what he felt for her was a
certain pity. It seemed she could survive well enough
without any friends, but he was sure that deep down she
didn't really want it to be that way. In part it was because
of the kiss that night, and the fact he knew for certain she
had enjoyed it.

Still, he was determined not to be the one to make the
first move. He had done that too many times before, he
figured, and look where it had gotten him. This time he was
sure he had the willpower to see it through.

Even so, he was surprised when one day after recess he
found a note on his desk that was signed N. She had

written that she needed to talk to him and asked if they could get together some night that weekend. He could hardly believe that she had written it. He glanced back. For that second she was staring straight into his eyes and smiling. He knew then it had to be her. It was the most straightforward look she had ever given him and it stayed with him all through school that day.

He jumped at the chance to spend time with her again. After school he went up to her while she was standing by her locker and mentioned Saturday night and asked if that would be a good time. She said it was perfect.

He was sorry afterward that he had sounded so eager, but the regret didn't stay with him for long. All he could really think about was what they might be doing together on Saturday night.

A second note showed up on his desk the next day. It said, "Come to my house around eight." She had a small map drawn showing exactly where it was. He knew already.

At seven forty-five on Saturday night he was standing on the side of the main road, at the end of the path that led to her house. He had noticed the house lots of times while driving through Spencer's, but he seemed to remember it being boarded up, at least during the winter. A lot of houses along the bank were old like that one and used only as summer homes, mostly by people who lived the rest of the year in St. John's.

Like the others along the road, it looked out over the bay. A stiff wind blew off the saltwater, causing David to check his watch and wish it were closer to the time she had set. He sheltered himself against a large poplar that grew near the road. The garden in front of the house was thick with old apple trees and berry bushes that had been left to grow wild.

The house was two-story and box-shaped, the same as

most of the older houses around. Like the garden, it had seen better days. It looked solid enough, but it hadn't been painted for many years. In the dimness of the streetlight, it looked as if it had a past that nobody cared about anymore.

David could see a light on upstairs and another over the back porch. He knocked at the back door at exactly eight o'clock. Nancy was at the door, opening it wide for him, before he needed to knock a second time. He hurried inside out of the cold.

As they walked together into the light and the warmth of the kitchen, he was struck by how beautiful she looked. Her black hair shone. A touch of red color in her cheeks and on her lips softened her eyes. It made him stare at her until she took away his attention by passing him a hanger for his coat.

"Sorry," he said. "It's just that I haven't seen you look like this before."

A lot of girls, he knew, would have blushed. She accepted it without any reaction at all. He put his coat on the hanger, but all the while he was looking at what she was wearing. It was the first time he had ever seen her in a dress. It was dark green, the color of forest moss, and made of a thin material that looked like it had the feel of suede. It hung loose and slim. In front, on the right side just below her shoulder, was a single caribou embroidered in beads. She looked beautiful.

"Go in the living room. I'll be there in a minute." She pointed to a closed door at the other end of the kitchen, then disappeared with his coat.

It struck him as odd that there should be a door and it would be closed. As soon as he opened it, the reason was all too clear. Cold air swept over him, sending a shiver through his body. It wasn't much warmer than it was outdoors. Vapor clouded the air when he breathed.

He would have gone back into the kitchen but for the wood stove in the room. It wasn't lit, but its front doors were open and there was a pile of split wood nearby. He walked over and sat on the edge of the sofa, as near as he could to the stove. He was just about to start putting in wood to make a fire when Nancy came in.

"A bit chilly for you," she said, laughing. He hadn't heard her laugh so freely before.

She knelt down in front of the open doors of the stove, and taking one piece of wood at a time, she arranged several of them inside.

"I'll get some newspaper," he said.

"That's okay." She tore thin strips of birch bark from the wood that remained. She positioned them carefully among the pieces of wood in the stove. David handed her a box of matches from the end table near the sofa.

"A great convenience — matches," she said.

She lit one and set it to the birch bark. As the flames rose to a blaze she quickly added three or four pieces of kindling, being careful to place them so they would take full advantage of the flames without smothering them. She left the doors open, but fitted a screen to the front of the stove.

She sat in an armchair across from him. Both of them stared at the fire. David edged forward as much as he could without falling off the sofa. He stretched out his hands and rubbed them together. He still felt the chill throughout his body. He couldn't keep from shivering. And he couldn't get over the fact that, although there were goose bumps on her arms, the cold didn't seem to be bothering her in the least.

She smiled. "Just as I thought. Your body has been pampered."

It didn't bother him what she said. Just the fact that she was talking and smiling and looking like she was having a good time was enough in itself.

"Sure," he said, smiling too.

"My family would have laughed at you."

"Are they here?"

"Not now," she said quickly.

She stood up and walked to the wall near the door. Her hand adjusted a thermostat. Then she returned to the armchair, as if there had been no reason before to have done it.

He still had his eyes on her, expecting more about her family.

"It's not something I really want to talk about."

He looked away.

"Strange house," he said. "Seems so cold and empty."

"It's not always like that."

He looked around the room. The furniture was old and worn and some of it needed repair. A few pieces looked like they might be antiques. The floor was hardwood, covered here and there with hooked mats like those he had seen in old pictures of his grandparents' house. Heavy, faded drapes covered the windows.

What he found most interesting were the pictures on the walls. There were several of stern-looking men and women dressed in clothes that must have come from another century. The pictures were in heavy wooden frames. He was just about to ask who they were when Nancy stood up again.

"Would you like something to eat?" she asked.

"Why not."

After she left the room he walked over to look at the pictures more closely. He stopped for a moment at each one, then walked along to what turned out to be an old framed map of Newfoundland, dated 1790. A lamp on the table under it gave plenty of light to see it clearly.

It showed the island a lot broader than it really was, and not so detailed in its coastline. He searched the area where

Marten would have been if it had existed then. What he found were the names of the islands off the coast that he had heard his grandfather use when he talked about the years before he and his family moved to Marten. Nobody lived in these places anymore. He remembered the old man saying that the house where he had been raised had rotted and fallen down.

Nancy walked back into the room carrying a tray. On it was a plate covered with thin slices of smoked salmon. David was surprised. Smoked salmon didn't come cheap.

"What are you looking at?" she asked.

"Red Ochre Island. Remember I mentioned it to you before. That's where my grandparents lived one time, where the skeleton was found." He pointed to it on the map.

"I'd like to go there sometime, wouldn't you?" she said, not bothering to look at the map. "Just to see what it's like. I think it would be really interesting."

It caught him by surprise. "I hadn't really thought about it. I mean, I've heard my grandfather talk about the place lots of times, but I've never really wanted to go, I guess. Until now."

"Do you think it's hard to get to?"

"Not really. Not if you had a boat."

"Canoe?"

He laughed. "Too rough. Unless it was a real calm day. I meant motorboat."

"I'd say you could do it in canoe."

"Maybe. But you'd be taking chances."

She shrugged. "Not if you went downriver." She pointed it out on the map. "It's not far from the mouth of the river to the island."

"I guess."

"Perhaps we should do it sometime."

He could hardly believe it. An invitation for the two of

them to go somewhere out of the way like that. Perhaps she didn't mean alone.

"Nobody would have to know."

He wasn't sure what to say.

"You don't want to?"

"Yeah, I want to. Sure."

"Good." She lifted the tray toward him. "Here, have some."

"I love smoked salmon. My grandfather smokes some every year." He took a cracker from the tray, placed two pieces of salmon on it and put the whole thing in his mouth.

They sat down side by side on the sofa. She put the tray down on the coffee table near them.

"Your grandfather fishes for salmon?" she asked.

"Yeah. He's got two nets he puts out."

He leaned forward and put some more of the salmon on a cracker and put it in his mouth. When he sat back he saw that her eyes were closed and her hand was against the side of her head.

"I get headaches sometimes," she said, before he had a chance to speak. "They come on really quickly. I'm okay."

"Can I get you something?"

She didn't answer. When she didn't move for a long time, he leaned back and stared silently at her bent figure next to him. At first he just sat there trying to think what he should be doing. After a while his eyes began to linger on the bareness of her neck, from her hairline to the edge of her dress. Smooth, brownish skin, gently indented by her spine. He found himself rubbing the thumb of one hand along the tops of his fingers. He wished he could have been running his fingertips along her neck.

She began to straighten up. He kept looking at her until he thought she was about to turn and look at him.

She didn't. She said, "Would you go upstairs to the

bathroom and get a cold cloth? Sometimes it helps."

He was on his feet right away. The stairs were through the archway that led out of the living room.

"At the far end of the hall."

He walked out of the room to the foot of the stairs. Light from the living room dimly covered the lower steps. He started up the stairs quickly, his hand sliding along the thick, heavily painted railing. But as he went higher, he had to slow down. He had moved out of the light and he could barely see the landing ahead. When he reached it, only the curve of the railing guided him around to the remaining steps.

It was dark, but for the first time all evening he felt warm. With each step the air became thicker with heat. The change was so sudden that for a moment he found it hard to breathe.

As he neared the top step he could see light at the end of the hallway. He stopped at the head of the stairs. It was a murky, clouded light coming from the half-opened door to the bathroom. He began to sweat heavily — from the heat, he reassured himself, not from any fear he felt as he slowly continued along the hall.

As he came closer to the bathroom he could see it was steam that was clouding the light. It drifted out like a thin fog from behind the partially opened door. He stopped and listened. Someone taking a hot bath? No sound.

From where he stopped, he could see the sink and a facecloth lying next to one of the taps. It was so close to the door that it looked to him as if he should be able to stretch in his arm and get it without having to enter the room.

He looked around him. All the other doors along the hall were closed. He looked back to the head of the stairs. Only the top of the railing was visible. He hadn't come this far to go back empty-handed, he told himself.

He listened again. Nobody taking a bath could be that

quiet. The thought struck him that someone might emerge from one of the other rooms, heading for the bathroom.

Suddenly—the sound of the light being switched on in one of the rooms behind him. He twisted around and saw a band of light under one of the closed doors between himself and the stairway.

He rushed ahead, and bracing himself with one hand on the facing of the doorway, he stretched his other hand inside to the sink and closed it over the cloth.

At that instant a horribly hard, rasping cough cut through the steam! He hauled his hand back like he had touched fire.

He rushed back down the hall, past the still unopened door. He caught himself with the railing at the head of the stairs, jerking his speed in half.

He raced down two unseen steps at a time, until he reached the landing. He forced himself to stop. His heart was pumping madly. In the dim light he walked down the rest of the steps.

At the bottom of the stairs he stopped again. He put his hand to his chest. He kept it there until he felt his heartbeat slow down.

He went back into the living room, his breathing still heavy. As he got near the sofa he could see that Nancy was lying across the full length of it. He held out the cloth to her. For the first time he realized it was wet and cold as it needed to be.

She took it. "Is there something wrong?" she asked.

"I thought we were alone in the house?"

"I didn't say we were. Did something frighten you?"

"You might say that. Scared the hell out of me, actually."

She laughed at him like he was overreacting. "I thought you would have learned by now not to be surprised when you're with me."

She closed her eyes and lay the cloth across her forehead.

He stared at her for a long time, expecting her to eventually open her eyes again and talk to him. Instead, she seemed to be drifting off to sleep.

Now he felt alone, an intruder almost. He kept glancing in the direction of the stairs. For a while he sat in the armchair where she had first been sitting. Then he got up and went to look for his coat. He found it in a closet off the kitchen, hung up next to her old fur coat. He put on his coat and then took hers from the hanger and carried it into the living room. He spread it over her, the fur side to her body. She was sound asleep.

He stood back and stared at her for a few seconds. He wanted to stand there longer, but he kept thinking he could hear something move upstairs.

He knelt down on one knee and gave her a kiss on her cheek. She stirred, but did not open her eyes. Still looking at her, he stood up and zippered his coat. He left her there and quickly found his way outdoors.

Dauoodaset

When it is the morning to leave I feel a great excitement that I have not known before. The sky holds only thin trails of clouds like smoke. The sun when the full of its face is shown will be clear and bright and strong. A mist, like what rises from animal flesh killed in winter, drifts in silence above the water of the river as I get ready my canoe.

It is only me that does not sleep. I have been awake at the first feel of light for many mornings. I have risen and crawled through the door flap of the mamateek out into the chilled air to look at the sky. For many mornings there was no hope of going and I crawled back into my sleeping pit full of bad feelings.

But it is not so today. Soon I will begin the journey that will take me to the end of suffering for my people. I had fear that I would grow myself too weak with hunger to make the journey and would lie helpless while the winds blew cold and forced my canoe to stay on the land.

I turn the canoe from its resting place on the bank and lift it to where it lies with one end in the water and the other holding to the land. I place the flat stones that I gathered many days ago along the bottom of the canoe to hold it steady for paddling. Where I will be kneeling I put moss over the stones. I try it to be sure that there are no sharp edges of stone to give me pain for the long days of my paddling.

Now my canoe lies ready. I go back to the mamateek to gather what is there for me to take and to tell the others that this is the day. Only Waumaduit has heard me. From the quickness of my moving about the mamateek, she knows that I will be going. She is not so weak that she does not worry about her son. In her heart she feels the danger ahead for me, but she knows I am the strongest hope for our people.

She sits now in her resting pit. She tells me in a whispering voice of a pouch that I must take with me and where I must go to find it.

"When you grow weary and have no strength to move for paddling, then open the pouch," she says. "It will bring to you the courage to go on when you think you cannot."

I draw close to my mother. It hurts to see her face so thin, her hair hanging untidy about it. I have heard her cough now in the nights and I think the worst and hope it is not true. I hold her close to me and we sing together one of the songs, as we used to do when I was younger.

She helps me then as I put red ochre over my body. "Do not worry," I tell her. "I will be safe. Think only of the good times there will be when again we are together."

Some of the others have stirred at the sound of our voices. It is for me now to tell them that I am ready to make my start. There are words of hope for a plentiful journey and words of warning not to use all my strength in the eagerness to get there.

My father rises and comes to my side. He holds in his hand the spear which his father before him used at the great hunts of long ago. I have never seen it thrown but from the hands of my father. He takes my hand and presses it tight around the spearshaft. When he looks at my face it is not with a smile, but with a look of pride drawn tight with worry.

Shamoonon comes by me and wishes me good fortune. When I look at him I am glad he is not going on the journey. I tell him I will bring back many mussels, his favorite, for all the help he has been to me.

It is Edeshnon now who stands tall against the side of the mamateek. His voice holds still some of the power of the days he led us to this place by the river. "Dauoodaset," he speaks. "You are young. You are going to do what we all would do if there was not the age in our bones. You will meet hardship on your way and your body will know pain from the burden we have passed to you. Remember well the faces of our people. Think hard on them and they will give you the strength you will need."

I know Old Man does not speak for all of them. The choice of his words is his own. I do not feel anger. It is a pride I feel, a feeling of fight in my blood that will make him sorry he doubts what I can do.

I tell them all, "I will return with my canoe filled with the meat of many fish and animals. Hold to my face in your thoughts and think of the time when I return and to the time we will paddle together to the saltwater."

As I leave the mamateek with my things to take, Waumaduit tells me to have some strong tea drink before I go. Outside I heat some water and do as she says. I find the pouch which she has hidden for me, and now I make my way to where the canoe waits. I look back only once.

I lay in my canoe the furs of my resting pit. They are my guard against the cold of the night when there will be no mamateek to break the wind. My spear and my bow and my store of arrows lie close to where I kneel. They must be quick to my hand for the kill of any animal that I might see

David

All during the next week David tried to decide if he should follow up on Nancy's hint that they make a trip to Red Ochre Island together. Just as he expected, there was no explanation for what had happened on Saturday night. When they talked, it was as if nothing out of the ordinary had taken place. He wouldn't mention how frightened he had been for fear she'd think he was being childish about it. He began to wonder if really he hadn't imagined some of it. Or at least imagined it to be worse than it really was.

Nancy was friendlier than ever. In fact, she was going out of her way to be nice to him, something just a few weeks before he couldn't have imagined her doing. He found it strange, but no stranger than a lot of other things she did.

He had given up on trying to make sense of everything about her. Why not just go along with it and enjoy it for whatever it was? At least he wasn't bored. Maybe it would all turn out to be worth it in the end, now that he was sure she had some pretty strong feelings for him too.

He went to bed Friday night thinking about all that. He woke up the next morning with other things on his mind.

He lay in bed wondering about himself and the old man. When he finally got out of bed it was after eleven.

A few minutes later he walked into the kitchen. His mother was looking through a magazine and drinking tea.

"Where is everybody?"

"Your father and Brad are in the woods. Sandra is gone somewhere with one of her friends."

"He should have called me," he said, putting some bread in the toaster. "Perhaps I'll go and find them after I get something to eat."

His mother looked up. She didn't say anything.

"Where's he cutting? In back of Black Duck Pond?"

"I believe so," she said. "Put on plenty of clothes. It's not all that warm out."

He gave her a sour look, exaggerated to the point that she smiled.

"I'm still your mother," she said.

Outside later, with the temperature hovering around the freezing mark, he walked for a couple of miles along the main road and then down a side road to where the pickup was parked. Nearby was the path which ran to Black Duck Pond and a large pile of spruce in seven- and eight-foot lengths. He could see that a steady run of a Ski-doo back and forth through the path had beaten down what was left of the snow. From the look of the pile he could tell that they were hauling out wood that had just been cut.

Rather than walk in to meet them, he decided to sit on the pile and wait for someone to show up with the next load. He didn't have long to wait, although the cold was starting to get to him by the time he heard the distant roar of the Ski-doo.

It was Brad. He had guessed right. Brad stopped the Ski-doo so that the load he was hauling on the sleighs behind was in line with the pile David was sitting on.

Brad looked surprised to see him.

"Thought I'd come in and give you guys a hand," David said.

"Sure."

"It's friggin' cold."

"Go on," Brad said, teasing. "You're soft."

David made a motion to grab him. Brad didn't back off, just laughed.

Brad untied the chain that was wrapped around the load, and they stood one at each end of the wood and tossed it piece by piece onto the pile. It was heavy work.

"Try unloading them by yourself sometime," Brad said, seated sideways on the Ski-doo now. He had one mitt off and the top half of his Ski-doo suit unzipped. He reached under his sweater to his shirt pocket and took out a cigarette.

"You smoke?" David said.

"Now and then. Mom don't know. And don't tell her."

"What about the old man?"

"I don't smoke in front of him. But I daresay he knows."

David left it at that. When Brad had finished his cigarette and had flicked the butt into a patch of snow, he started up the Ski-doo again. He turned in a circle around the pile of wood and headed the Ski-doo back toward the path to the pond. David jumped on behind him, and they took off together, the empty sleighs trailing behind. The path was bare of snow in places, and in some it had softened to mud. Even over these, Brad drove as hard as he could. Bumps in the path jolted David from the seat again and again, and once he nearly went flying off. Only when they got near to where the old man was cutting did Brad slow down. He looked behind and grinned at David.

"Jerk!" David yelled at him above the noise of the engine.

The path turned into a steep climb. The Ski-doo lost more and more speed, until finally David had to get off to keep it from bogging down. He stood to one side of the path and watched as his brother rocked the Ski-doo from side to side to get it to the top of the hill.

David walked behind. By the time he made it over the crest of the hill he was out of breath. He looked along the path to where the Ski-doo was stopped and to where the old man was standing. A chain saw hung from his right hand. David straightened up and walked toward them slowly to give himself time to get his breath back.

"C'mon," Brad yelled. "Don't be such a wimp."

They stood there almost motionless until David reached them. He looked from one to the other and then to the woods around.

"Thought I'd come in and give you guys a hand," he said to the old man.

"Sure," the old man said. He wiped his forehead with the sleeve of his sweater. He swung the chain saw up and let it drop again. "Well," he said, "back to work. I'll finish up what I was at. You fellows can haul out another load." He walked back over the snow to where he'd been cutting.

David didn't wait for Brad to make the first move. He started the Ski-doo and sat aboard. With Brad behind him shouting directions, he set off to the pile of wood to be loaded.

They made two trips together to the roadside. David took out a third load on his own. He had a hard struggle to get the wood off by himself, but he didn't stop to rest after it was done.

When he got back, the old man was sitting by a fire, waiting for water to boil for tea. Brad was not far away, taking target practice with an old gun belonging to his father. When he noticed David, he put the gun back in its case and came over to the fire.

"Sit down," the old man said to David, "and have a rest."

"We don't want them muscles of yours to get strained," Brad said, sitting down himself on some boughs that were piled near the fire.

"I'll strain a few knuckles around your mouth if you don't keep quiet."

"Scare me, why don't ya."

There were boughs enough for them both. David sat down and leaned forward.

"It's gettin' too mild," the old man said. "We'll soon have to give this up for the day."

The water began to boil in the large can they were using for a kettle. "Fire in the tea bags," Brad said.

There were only two mugs. The old man passed around an open can of peach halves with a spoon. When they were all eaten he drained out what juice was left and used the can as a mug for himself. All three of them were sipping on hot tea and eating bread toasted in the fire.

"Nothin' like it," the old man said.

David was beginning to relax a bit. He wrapped his hands tightly around the mug and leaned back.

"This is the life," Brad said.

"Don't get too comfortable," his father told him. "You might end up at this for the rest of your life."

"That wouldn't be so bad."

"You get your education like I told ya."

"Not this again," Brad said, rolling his eyes.

David was surprised at that coming from the old man. He had heard his mother get on Brad's back lots of times for not being interested in school. But he had the feeling that when the old man and Brad were together, they never had anything to argue about.

"If you had half the interest in school your brother's got . . ."

That was enough to make David smile at the old man, then laugh out loud when he said that Brad should have his brain tuned up, or better still, traded in for a new one.

"You guys," Brad said, "make me sick."

On their way back home they stopped off at his grandfather's house. As long as David could remember, the only thing he ever called him was Pop. That hadn't changed after he found out that he wasn't really his grandfather. He had thought a lot about it, and he knew he didn't feel much different about him.

The three of them threw off some birch from the box of the pickup, as his grandfather looked out from the back door.

"Not much of a day out in boat," his grandfather said.

"Not fit," the old man told him. "Goin' out Monday now, if 'tis civil. There's a few birds on the go yet, accordin' to what they're sayin'. If I can get another day at 'em, I'll be satisfied."

"Any sign o' seals?"

"What's the use? Nobody's buyin' pelts. I had enough for a few meals. I'm not wastin' me time at it."

"Make you sick. They got it ruined, that animal welfare crowd. There's poor devils in Africa starvin' to death, and here they is kickin' up a stink about us fellows making a few dollars."

It was a topic that his grandfather could really get fired up about. It made David think twice about staying behind to talk to him. He knew that sometimes, once he got going on one thing, it was hard as hell to get him to talk sensibly about anything else.

But he decided he'd take the chance. "You guys go on," he told the others, after the wood was unloaded and they were sitting in the pickup. "I'll walk back."

His grandfather was glad to have the company. They sat together at the kitchen table. Heat from the wood stove nearby forced David out of his heavy coat and sweater.

"Pop, you got it hot enough to roast a pig."

"Sure, when I was a boy, seals was half we lived on in the spring o' the year. Yes, it was." David let him talk without saying much back to him, hoping that he might wear himself down.

When it seemed to fit, David said, "The same thing about the Beothuks. There are people saying now that some of the settlers back then were nothing but a bunch of barbarians for the way they treated them."

"The Beothuks is a different story. If you ask me, no one knows the rights o' that. I heard stories when I was a boy, but who knows what to believe and what not to believe."

"What stories?"

"I hardly knows, it's that long ago now. There was one on Red Ochre Island one time, I knows that for a fact. Me grandfather showed me some bones when I was a boy. Showed me where he found them. I daresay there's not much left there now."

"Yeah," David said, eager for more. "What else did he say?"

"People used to say that's how the place got its name. The Indian who died there was covered in red ochre. But you can't go by that. Nobody'll ever know the rights of it, it was that long ago."

David wanted to dig further, to get all he could out of him while the going was good.

"There might be bones still there, you never can tell," David said.

"Could be. I daresay if someone was willing to look hard enough, they might come up with something. Take a trip yourself sometime and see what you can find."

His grandfather told him where on the island the bones had been found. But try as David did to get more details, there just wasn't any more his grandfather could tell him. He started to repeat what he had said already. David let him drift off to talking about something else.

When he got up to go, Pop said he really wished he could stay a while longer. But it was already dark and David said that his mother was no doubt wondering if he was ever going to show up for supper. He promised his grandfather that he'd be back before long.

He walked home along the main road in Marten, the one he had walked thousands of times before. He knew every corner of this place, he was telling himself, every house and every person in them. He used to look through walls and imagine what they were saying, and who they were saying it about. Before the trip into St. John's he'd been thinking how much he wanted to get away from Marten, to be somewhere where nobody knew who he was.

Maybe, he was thinking now, it would be just as easy to laugh about the way they gossiped. Make jokes about it. They were no better than he was. And they had their secrets. Some of them probably a lot worse than his own.

Dauoodaset

The first night of my journey has come and I am happy that I have gone far. I think it is much longer that I have to go, but if all days pass so quickly it will be soon that I will find it at an end.

The night is a cold one. I have made a place to sleep near the fire. The canoe I have turned over to cover me. It does not keep out the frost like the mamateek, so I hold myself tightly in the furs and keep wood to the fire. I cannot have my muscles turn stiff.

The hunger that I have known for many days is still with me. It is now a hard pain in my stomach. River water boiled and steeped with leaves for drink makes some of the pain go away. I tried to keep my eyes sharp as I paddled for sign of animal or fish. I saw once the running of some animal through the trees, but there was no hope of a kill. Soon I will have to take daylight and look for food. I cannot be wanting to go too fast and use all my strength so that I have none for hunting. For now I chew the inside bark of the birch and hold my mind to the good start of my journey. Sleep comes quickly.

In the morning the cold stays in the air. There is no

bright sun like the day before and wind blows across the canoe, making it hard to paddle. It is now that I wish there was another with me to make less work.

Before I have gone far, flakes of snow wild with the wind are beating down on me. At first I paddle on, doing all that I can do against it. Soon I am tired and I look back and see that I am not far from the place on the bank where I started. I cannot waste my strength this way. It is better that I wait until the wind is passed. I pull the canoe on the shore and turn it for shelter from the blowing snow. I cover myself with furs and sit with my legs tight to my chest and wait. It is cold and I am in misery.

It is here that I stay until it is dark again, and then until it is daylight the next morning. Many times during the night I thought of the pouch that Waumaduit filled for me. Many times I wanted to open it, for the cold and the hunger were like none that I knew before. I did not. There may be many days when I will need it more.

I stand on the shore this morning, stiff and weary. The wind has gone. There is no more snow to fall. I wish only to start again and put what has happened out of my mind. I fight at the pains that I feel in my bones. They all do not go away. There is a bend in my back that was not there before and a soreness in my shoulders when I raise up my arms.

The snow lies in patches among the clumps of dead grass. Where there is no grass, it has blown away. I look to see if there are any nests of birds, but I know before I look that it is not the way of birds to be so early.

I think that I must not waste daylight in a search for nothing. But then I see in the snow the fresh tracks of an otter. My heart quickens. As fast as I can move my stiffened body, I run to where the canoe lies and get my bow and its arrows. When I return it is with great slowness. I move close to the ground and find a place where small trees hide me. It is there that I wait. It is a long wait and the cold comes again into my bones.

But the spirits have for me all that I pray for. An otter darts again along the path that it made. It stops and rises on its back legs. It is long enough for my arrow to find a way to its body. It is not the shot to kill it, for I did not have the eye to shoot as I wished. The otter drags itself away. But I am quick to it and with the wood of my bow I smash its head until it moves no more.

I cannot believe what I have done. It makes me cry to think that again I will know the taste of meat.

I find a place among the taller trees for a fire. There is little wind, and the dead sticks burn with a strong heat. The flesh of the otter is still warm when I pierce it with a stick and hold it to the fire. And when my teeth sink into it I am crying for joy and for the thought of my people who cannot share my good fortune.

I know better than to eat all that I have before me. My body will need time to know again the feel of meat. It is better that I save most of it for boiling into soup. I wrap my precious store in the skin of the birch and return to my canoe.

It is a new start I make. I have a new hope that the promises I have made to my people will be brought to them. I will have the strength to take my journey to its end.

My heart is glad. The winter cold goes once again. And the feel of the sun on my face brings with it a smile. Shanawdithit travels again with me and I know that she is holding me in her thoughts.

David

It got so that some others in the class were beginning to think of David and Nancy as a lot more than just friends. Some of the guys started to kid him about it. It was true, she did spend very little time talking with anyone else. She was nice enough when others in the class spoke to her, but it never got to the kind of personal conversations that she had with him.

For the first time he was positive that she liked him. Now when they talked, she often said things that had come fresh to her mind, that didn't seem planned, like so much of what had gone on between them before.

He wanted them to get together on the weekend. This time somewhere other than her house. The easiest way to ask her would have been over the phone, but the phone where she was living still hadn't been hooked up. A note seemed too impersonal now. It would have to be face-to-face. The trouble was, they were hardly ever really alone in school. He thought of going over to her house and asking her there, but he wasn't sure she would appreciate that. After thinking his way through all the possibilities, he decided he'd make some excuse to get her to go to the library with him. There, maybe, they could get far enough away from other people that he could ask her.

He went up to her at recess and asked if she had her paper on the Beothuks finished.

"All except the final part."

"Me too. I'm not sure how to end it. Got time to come up to the library? I want to ask you something about one of the books I used."

"Sure."

The way she was being so agreeable all the time, almost going out of her way to be nice to him, did make him wonder if she wasn't suddenly going to snap back to the way she was before. But maybe she had really changed. And maybe, he liked to think, his stubbornness in hanging around her was part of the reason for that change.

In the library he led her to where the history books were shelved. He had guessed right. There was nobody else within hearing range.

"What I really want to know is — can we get together this weekend?"

For a second she didn't quite realize that his only reason for bringing her there was to see if she would go out with him, that he wasn't going to take down a book and ask her something about it. When it did strike her, she looked upset for a second, but then she covered it with a grin.

She said, "Sure."

David was hoping for something more. And the way she had said it sounded to him like she had something else on her mind.

"Great," he said, with about the same amount of enthusiasm.

She seemed to sense his disappointment.

"What will we do?" she asked, sounding a lot more interested.

He couldn't tell if it was for real or not. But it was better than her saying no. And a few weeks before, that's just what she would have done.

"There's a good movie on. But I'm open to suggestions."

"It doesn't really matter to me."

"I'll come by your place about eight o'clock on Saturday."

"Great."

He thought afterward, when he was trying to concentrate on his work in math class, that maybe he was expecting too much too soon. Things had changed a lot between them, it was true. And maybe this date would change things even more. He should be thankful for that much. Who knew anyway what was going on in her mind that she wasn't telling anyone about.

That Saturday night they met at exactly eight. She must have been watching for him, because as soon as he started up the path toward her house, she came out the back door dressed to go. Even though it was more springlike now, and almost all the snow had gone, she was still wearing the fur coat that she had been wearing all winter. He didn't say anything about it, but he knew they must have looked odd together with him wearing his school jacket.

"Where will we go? The movie?"

"What else is there?"

"The hangout. And some of the crowd are going over to Karen's. Her parents are gone for the weekend. We could go there."

There weren't a whole lot of choices of things to do in Marten. He didn't mention going to one of the guys' cabins in the woods and drinking beer, which was the only other possibility he knew of.

"The movie."

They talked constantly all the way to the main road. Mostly they talked about the trip she had proposed they

"I didn't mean what I said. I wasn't thinking," she said, still not looking directly at him.

He was determined that he wasn't just going to let her have it all her own way, like the other times. He still wouldn't say anything.

Then she looked at him, directly into his eyes. He wasn't going to have her pull that one on him again. He turned away.

"The two of us . . . it's not going to work," he said.

She forced her way into his line of vision.

"Don't say that. I'm sorry about what happened. I really am."

She put her arms around him and held on to him tightly, her head against his shoulder. He remained stiff and unyielding.

She was acting all the world like she needed him. When she let go and looked at him again, he could feel his anger slowly melting away. He knew he wasn't going to be anything but forgiving.

He squeezed her and told her that it was okay, that if he had known it was going to bother her so much, they never would have gone.

They held each other for a long time. He felt like kissing her, but her face stayed buried in his shoulder. They broke apart when a pair of headlights came toward them.

They walked together back to her house. Neither one of them said much, but to David there was a tenderness between them that wasn't there before. The angry words had cleared the air.

They stood at the back entrance to her house for a long time. They talked quietly. At times, when she was not saying anything, he wasn't sure what she had on her mind, but the way she was looking at him made him feel certain that it was about him and that it was good.

She didn't invite him inside. He hadn't expected her to.

What he did expect and got was a long, lingering kiss before he left. When their lips parted and he looked at her, she was smiling warmly.

"Goodnight," she said. "We'll get together during the week and make plans for Saturday."

He had almost forgotten about Saturday. Something now to really look forward to.

"Sure."

The kiss lingered in his mind all the way home.

Dauoodaset

I have slept three nights under my canoe. I do not think it can be much longer. I have eaten the flesh of the otter and, after it, eels that came near the shore in the light of my fire to steal away the guts of the otter. The food has taken from me some of the ache in my stomach. I feel strength where I have not known it for many days. It will keep me to the end of my journey, to where the saltwater holds all it has for me.

Only now have I come to a place where I cannot paddle. Far before it I heard the change of water sounds. I paddled along the shore to where the water crashes and falls long over the rocks. It is safe only to carry the canoe through the trees to the pool below. I went first with the bow and its arrows and the other things, to find the best way to go for carrying the canoe.

The way is hard. The trees are many together and it is steep. I watch that the branches do not catch the canoe and pierce its skin. I watch too that the bending past the trees does not crack its sewing and cause it to leak.

When I reach the pool below I have to rest for a long while, for now I must find new rocks and new moss to lay in the bottom of the canoe. There are not the good flat rocks for me to find. When I start again my paddling, the canoe does not hold so steady in the water, but I see no place to search for other rocks. The end of the river cannot be far. When I reach the saltwater there will be all the rocks that I will need.

It is good to be inside the canoe again. I hold the paddle still except to steer and let the rush of the water below the falls carry me away. I rest until the river once more is wide. Now the paddling begins again. The sun shines strong, enough that now I sweat and have to shed some of my furs. I think of my hunter-thanking song and I sing it as I go. My heart too sings.

The words stop. My heart quickens. There is a turn in the river, and when I look as far as I can see, there is water so wide I know it must be the saltwater. Can this be the end? I shout out the words of my song!

I think back to the journey I have made and I know that I will have the strength to get back to my people. They will know the truth of the promises I have made. Old Man will know that my ways are right. It is I who will have saved my people.

I begin to paddle harder. My strokes are long, but quick. The trees pass faster and faster. The words of my hunter-thanking song fly high to the spirits. So loud that Shanawdithit will hear me.

I am at the place where the river flows into the sea. A short way ahead I see an island. Birds fly in circles over it. They are a good sign. It is there that I will go first to gather food to fill the canoe. My paddle sinks deep into the water. I sing out to those birds.

Suddenly, I stop! My heart sinks. Just ahead of my canoe I see what I hoped I would never see — a net stretched across the river!

I look quickly about me to the banks of the river, but I can see no one.

As my canoe comes near to the net, I see the silver flash of many salmon caught in it. The whitemen have come again to rob us of our food!

There is anger like a knot tight in all my body. I will be quick and cut away the net and take what belongs to us.

A sound like thunder cracks the air! Something strikes the water near my paddle. My body goes stiff with fright.

It has come from behind bushes on the shore. When I look to them I see smoke rising. Before I have heard such a sound. As a boy near our camp. When my grandfather died. It is the sound of a whiteman's gun!

I paddle as fast as ever I can away from it and out to the sea. I must get to the island.

I must not lose my life. Not for me, for my people. I paddle with every bit of strength I have, harder and harder.

I am near to the island. Gunfire again! So close by me it makes me lose my balance. I fall from the canoe. I grab at my bow and arrows and my hunting spear. My bedding furs sink heavy with the water.

When I stand there is water to my waist. Gunfire once more! Water sprays around me, but I have not been hit by the whiteman's gun. I struggle toward the shore, dragging my canoe half sunk with water behind me. I pull it onto the shore and run to the trees for hiding.

I cannot think that this has happened to me. I am shivering from cold with nothing to warm me. My heart is cold. I am like running water that has turned to ice.

I can see a whiteman with a gun standing up in a boat out from shore. He is shouting words that have no meaning. Why has he done this? I have not done harm to him. He is not a man. He is a devil that looks like a man.

He sits down in the boat. My eyes follow his paddling. He is coming now to find where I hide!

I am crouched in the bushes quivering with cold and with fear.

David

She certainly meant what she said. It was the first thing she mentioned when he talked to her on Monday morning—the trip to Red Ochre Island. Had he thought about it some more? Had he made up his mind about the best way to get there?

Now it seemed definite that they were going, it was just a matter of straightening out the details. That didn't bother him much. He had spent a lot of Sunday thinking about Nancy and what it was that was keeping them together. He wasn't sure it was very much. And he made up his mind that the coming weekend he was going to find out a few things about her that he had to know. Like her background. Like why she was so strange sometimes and then really nice to him other times. What did she honestly feel about him anyway? He had to know. It was no use in going on like they were.

He had thought some more about using the canoe to get there. They could take the canoe up to where the highway crossed the river and paddle down to the mouth, like she had said. Then it would only be a quarter mile of open water from there to the island. If there was too much wind to get across in the canoe they would always try borrowing a rowboat from one of the people who had cabins along the shore.

"Great," she said, really enthusiastic.

"One problem," he said. "Getting the okay from my parents."

"They'll let you go on the river."

"Probably."

"Then don't tell them about the island. They won't need to know."

She was so definite about that. Like nothing should get in the way of their going.

"I guess so."

"You wouldn't really be lying. Just not telling them anything to get them worried."

It was settled, more or less. He'd ask one of his parents to take them up to the highway early in the morning. That was all he had to do, that and bring along the canoe. She said she could get someone to pick them up on Saturday evening before it got dark. And she insisted she would look after everything else — food, cooking gear, whatever they'd need.

He wasn't about to argue with that. That was the worst part of a canoe trip, getting ready for it.

"Just relax. I've thought of everything."

He wasn't sure what she meant by "everything." He didn't ask about the tent or sleeping bags. He couldn't be that bold. Not that it wasn't on his mind a lot.

As Saturday drew closer Nancy hung around him more and more at recess time and after school. They talked about other things, but the conversation always came around to the trip and whether or not he had made the arrangements with his parents. He kept telling her that there'd be no problem.

By Thursday he still hadn't gotten around to asking them. He stayed in after school to work out with the

117

weights by himself, and walking home alone he made up his mind that he would definitely do it when he got in the house.

The old man was on the couch looking like he had spent another long day in the woods. Brad and Sandra were sitting on the floor playing a game of cards and arguing over who had cheated. He sat down and watched television for a while without saying anything.

"Coming in the woods Saturday? We got to get the last of those logs to the mill," the old man said.

He was talking to him, not Brad. The way he asked it, like it wasn't anything special, caught him by surprise. He didn't want to say no. He explained that much as he'd like to, there really was a good reason why he couldn't. Then he told him about the trip.

"Can one of you drive us up?" David asked him. "We'll be going early, before you go in the woods."

"I guess so," he said.

"She's weird," Brad said. "I'd watch it if I were you. She might throw one of her screaming fits."

"Don't be such a friggin' jerk," David yelled at him.

The old man looked at David, but he didn't ask what Brad meant and he didn't say anything about Nancy. David was thinking the old man knew already that he was sort of going out with her.

"Just be careful, that's all. That water'll be freezin' cold this time o' the year. Take a change o' clothes and put it in something waterproof. And wear your life jackets."

Getting the okay from his mother was a different matter. She'd overheard part of what they were talking about, and when she came in the living room and he explained the rest of it to her, she looked at her husband like she wasn't so sure about it all.

"Don't worry. He'll be fine."

She didn't look convinced, but she didn't say anything.

David thought it was because the old man was on his side for a change and she wasn't about to argue with that.

"Really, I will. There's no place on the river that's very wide. Is there, Dad?"

His father agreed and she seemed to accept it. "I'll drive you up," she insisted. That would no doubt give her plenty of chance to hand out her warnings about being careful.

It was settled, then. The next day when he told Nancy, she couldn't hide her relief. She said she had all the other things ready. That she was glad her work wasn't wasted. He told her everything the old man had said about life jackets and keeping themselves dry and she agreed with all of it.

"Dad said we'll have to get going early 'cause he needs the truck."

"The earlier the better."

So they set the pickup time for seven thirty.

"I hope it'll be worth it."

She gave him a look that started as deeply serious in her eyes, then softened with a thin, devilish smile.

She was doing it to him again. He was starting to really look forward to Saturday.

Dauoodaset

Is it the fate of my people to die lying down in hunger about the mamateek, waiting for me? Will they die longing for the sight of my canoe?

The whiteman devil is coming toward the island with swift strokes of his paddles. He is careful not to come close to the woods where I squat, but he must know that I am quivering too much with the cold to hold straight my bow.

I am frozen like a fish on the ice in winter. I think that I will not move. Let me die before the rest of my people. Let me be there to meet them when they too come to the world of the spirits. I will tell them that I did all that I could do.

Then I think of my mother and my father and their words to me when I left the mamateek. And I look to the bone piece that hangs about my neck. I cannot come to death in this way. I must fight that whiteman devil until all that is in me is gone. I must die only when all of me is worn away.

The pouch that is my mother's gift is also about my neck. I pull at it with my stiffened hands until it is loose over my head. It is wound tight with cord. I chew hard at the cord with my side teeth and look, all the time watching with one eye the devil who nears the shore.

Finally it is free. But I stop and watch where he goes when his boat touches the shore. He lies low among the bushes with his gun pointed to the woods where I squat and then he runs into the tall trees. I pull open the pouch.

Inside are dried scraps of caribou meat. She must have held for me a secret store when she knew that I would make this journey. I think of Waumaduit and wish her to have it for her own body. I think of her sick and how it is that I may not see her again in this life. I will fight against my dying. I will drive arrows through the heart of that devil who comes after me.

Beneath the scraps are some dried leaves for steeping into drink. And beneath that are the best two of her firestones and the down feather of jay birds. She worried that I dressed warmly when I was with her, and I think now of the hot fire of the mamateek and the warmness of my furs in the resting pit. I know if I am to live I must have fire. I know too that it is the smoke of fire that will tell the whiteman devil where I lie.

I must move from this place before he gets too near. When I rise I am stiff and quivering so much that it is hard to hold the bow and its arrows. I listen for his noise, but my quivering makes it hard to hear. I will go slowly to where the trees are thick. It will be hard there for him to come without me to see him.

I see a flash of his clothes. I race to the trees. Gunfire cracks! His killing piece blows past my face. I fall flat to the ground, but there is no hit. I get up and race again. The trees hide me, but I know I cannot have so good fortune for many shots more.

And I cannot lie long in the trees. He will let me lie and freeze with the cold and die with no work of his gun. I must

When I stand in the open the wind blows cold on me again. I am weary. I want now to lie among the furs and rest my body and warm myself.

The furs are not dry. I drag them close to the fire and lie on them. I have nothing to cover me. I draw my body tight together like a child that is just born.

I think of my people. I think of Shanawdithit. My mind goes in circles about all that is still left to do. I hold to my hand the bone piece.

My body is heavy and still. I cannot force my eyes to open again. I drop away into sleep, where I feel the spirits calling to themselves all about me. I know that I must get wood for the fire to keep away the cold. The spirits will keep wood to the fire.

I am shivering no more. Shanawdithit draws me to the warmth of her body. She covers me. She makes me strong in my body again.

We hold together the life of my people. We are all that is left.

David

It was just before seven on Saturday morning when his mother woke him. He looked out the window. There was a light frost on the ground, but the sky was clear and it seemed as if it was going to stay that way. He looked at the trees. There was very little wind.

He dressed, had a quick breakfast, then went outside to load the canoe aboard the truck. Because they would be driving on the highway, he had to make absolutely sure that it was secure.

His mother started in on him as soon as they pulled out of the driveway. By the time they reached Spencer's Harbour she had him warned about every possible thing that could go wrong.

"You can never be too careful."

"Mom, don't worry. Trust me, I know what I'm doing."

As they approached Nancy's place they could see her at the side of the road, sitting on a knapsack, with a second one next to her. She was wearing her fur coat.

His mother glanced at him. She didn't say anything, but he could tell she was thinking that Nancy looked weird.

"She's really nice once you get to know her," he said.

"I'm sure she is," his mother said just as the pickup stopped. She left it at that.

Nancy had the knapsacks thrown aboard before he was out of the truck. He got back in and she sat beside him, near the window.

She retreated into her fur coat, almost as if it were a cocoon. She answered his mother's questions with a few words, and that was all she said. He wasn't surprised. He knew what she was like around people she didn't know. He was just wishing she'd let more of her intelligence show through. He got the feeling that his mother thought he had fallen for some half-brain who dressed funny.

As they came closer to where the river crossed the highway, Nancy started to get restless. She leaned her head forward, her eyes looking to all parts of the river. She had the door open the second the truck stopped. She walked straight to the water's edge and stood there motionless while David and his mother untied the canoe and dragged it to the shoreline.

A thin mist floated here and there over the water. When the sun grew stronger it would no doubt disappear. There wasn't any wind still. It was going to be a beautifully clear spring day.

When Nancy turned and looked at them, she was smiling. He was thinking it was the weather. But then he could see it had to be something much more than that.

His mother would have stayed longer, but she had promised that she would be right back with the pickup. He wished after that she could have stayed, to see them paddling together in the canoe. She would have been impressed with the way Nancy handled it.

Nancy had insisted on taking the stern, and after they started paddling, he saw why. It was if she had spent most of her life in one. He asked her where she had learned it all.

She didn't answer him.

She was more interested in deciding exactly where they were going. He wanted to take the canoe upriver first, if only to be able to say to his parents later that they did what he had said they were going to do.

She agreed, but she soon got tired of it and insisted that they were wasting valuable time. She had them turned around and heading downstream before he could put up much more of an argument. By then, after looking back at her and seeing the determination in the way she was paddling, he knew that it would have been useless to have said anything anyway.

Her mind was set on getting to that island. He glanced back at her several times. Each time her look seemed to be getting more intense. When he spoke to her, what she said was so mumbled it almost sounded like another language. At first he found it sort of funny, but then, when nothing he said seemed to get through to her, it started to really bother him.

"Slow down! What's the big rush?" he yelled at her.

Something must have clicked. Her head jerked up and then her face broke back to its familiar way of looking at him. He was relieved.

She even joked about how startled he had looked. He turned back, even more relieved, although still confused. They paddled quietly until they came to the mouth of the river.

Ahead of them they could see the island. There was no question in her mind that they were going to keep paddling. The sea to the island was almost flat calm, but he thought they should at least have talked about the chances of the wind coming up. She wouldn't give any thought to it. He said that maybe they should go over to one of the cabins and tell the people there where they were headed, just in case they did get stuck on the island and someone had to come looking for them. She started to paddle again, looking at him as if he didn't need an explanation.

"We have to get there," she said. "This is really going to be worth it."

He didn't have much choice. He could have insisted on doing things his way, but he knew it wouldn't have proven much. He was hoping instead that once they got to the island things would be different, that she would settle down and stop acting as if nothing he said mattered.

The trip across to the island was quick but uneventful. He didn't even look back at her, just tried to keep up with her stroke. When they neared land, she veered the canoe to the right, and around to the far side of the island. They paddled along the shoreline, past what was left of the old houses, until they came to a beach that she decided was the place where they had to haul up the canoe.

As soon as the canoe touched the beach she was up and climbing over the knapsacks, suddenly frantic to get out. She pulled at the bow of the canoe with him still in it, trying to get it farther up on the sand.

He jumped out. "What the hell's the matter with you?" He stood perfectly still and stared right at her.

She drew back. Her eyes shut and when she opened them she tried to look calm. But she was far from it. Her eyes darted about and would not stop to look directly at him. She couldn't keep still. Her hands rubbed up and down the fur of her coat.

He put his hands on her shoulders. She pushed them off and turned away from him.

"Nancy, what's with you? Look at me."

She wouldn't. She went off walking quickly along the beach.

He could see nothing to do but follow her. She walked faster and he had to run to try to catch up.

Then he noticed smoke rising in the distance. He had

taken for granted that they would be alone on the island. He stopped. He tried to think who it could be. A fisherman probably.

Nancy was running now, straight toward the smoke. The thought struck him that whoever it was might mistake the fur coat for an animal.

He ran faster. There was a shelf of rock a short distance in front of where the smoke was rising. Nancy disappeared over it.

He ran to the top of it. He could see to the beach below, to a tree, and to the fire.

He jerked to a stop. Nancy was near the fire, barefoot, her back to him.

And next to her a young man, long-haired, with fur about him too, but with bare patches of skin and his face colored red! In his hands he had a bow and arrow. It was aimed straight at David!

David's eyes sunk into his. Who in the name of God was it?

"Nancy!" he screamed out to her. "Nancy!"

Shanawdithit

He screams to me "Nancy." I am Nancy no longer. It is the whiteman's name. I am where I belong, with Dauoodaset. I am Shanawdithit.

I turn to his shouting, throwing wide the fur coat. I am wearing body furs like those of Dauoodaset and my arms and neck are colored red.

"I am Shanawdithit!" I call to him. I take the red of ochre and rub it over my hands and about my face. Dauoodaset's eyes shift from the aim of his bow to me and then back again.

He is wild with happiness at my coming to him. Others thought this island was the end for him, but it is not so. The life of our people will not be frozen away, never to walk about this land.

I stare at David. He is not the man like Dauoodaset. His hands are in the air, shaking with fear. I cannot have pity for him. The people from which he has come must feel the hurt they have done to us.

"Now you know the fear your ancestors drove into the hearts of my people! Now you suffer as they suffered. It was the first of your father's family who came to this land.

They took salmon with their nets and drove away our people with guns and killed them for no reason. This arrow can cut the life from you as bullets cut it from us. Think of the agony of this arrow into your flesh and then a knife slashed across your throat!"

His face is stiff. His eyes are bulging at me. I can look into those eyes now and see his ancestors and give him coldness as his people deserve. "Think on it, David."

He does not know what to think.

"It is your people who are the savages," I tell him.

He drops to his knees. He cries out, confused and filled with terror. "Nancy, you're playing crazy games with me!"

"I am Nancy no more. This is no game."

"Why are you doing this?" he pleads. "I don't know what's going on. We're friends. We came here to find out things for our assignment."

I smile the way he used to know. "We are Beothuks, Dauoodaset and I. Can you not see that?"

His body sinks lower. His hands are tight against his head. In time he will know that this is true.

Dauoodaset has been glancing at me with anxious looks. He is holding the bow rigid still. He slackens the arrow against the bowstring, but holds his aim. I smile at him and tell him in our language "Cockaboset," do not be afraid.

"Whadicheme?" he asks. Kill?

I think how David's ancestors killed my people, but I shake my head and tell him no.

I say to David, "Dauoodaset wants to know what to do with you. What did your father's people do to us who came down the rivers to the sea for food? Do you know?"

He does not answer.

I tell Dauoodaset to let down the bow. Then I tell David of Dauoodaset and all that has happened to him.

131

When I have finished there is a long quiet. David's eyes show he is thinking of many things. He has fear still for his life.

"The man you were talking about is not my father. I was born before my mother married him."

I have to think on this. He has said it like it is the truth.

"Does it matter? Those who let it happen were as shameful as those who pulled the triggers."

"You can't blame me for something that happened two hundred years ago!" he yells, desperate now.

"I am giving my people the chance they never had!" I yell back to him. "Where is there memory of my people? Skeletons in a museum. Bones and clothing and our precious neck pieces to gawk at. You saw them. They were of real people!"

He says nothing. He must know that what I speak is the truth.

I say to Dauoodaset that it is time to put away the bow and arrow. There is no need for David to have so much fear of us. I tell Dauoodaset that he has no weapons. Only then does he let the bow and arrow out of his hands. He lays them nearby so David can see that it would be useless to try to run away.

It is only now that I can look at Dauoodaset with the eyes of one who has longed so to be with him. I go to him and hold him against me. He draws my body tight to his and for a long time I think only of him and how glad I am that we are together. He is crying he is so happy. We are together as we are meant to be.

When finally we are apart, it is David's eyes I meet. He has the look of pain as before, but there is with him now another hurt. I cannot think he still has feelings for me. He must know that my love is for my people.

He looks away with bitterness. I feel pity now. But it is Dauoodaset that I must be with.

I tell David to walk ahead of us to where the fire is burning. He stands over it, taking into himself all the heat that he can. Dauoodaset throws more wood to the fire and now it burns so hot that we all have to move away. There are rocks nearby where we can sit.

I speak of the ocean and the mussels that are thick on the beach when the tide is low. I make him listen to stories of our people and how they loved to come to the saltwater in the spring of the year, like all their people before them. Then I tell him how his ancestors cut off their supply of food and stopped their coming.

David listens, but does not say anything. I can see that his fear of us is changing. There is not the terror in his eyes. Perhaps he sees some of me that he knew before. I am trying not to show it, but I cannot look at him without thinking of the way he treated me when others where he lived would have nothing to do with me. I have to get that out of my mind.

"Was I cruel to you?" he asks, looking long into my eyes.

He will not stop his staring at me.

"Look at me!" David shouts, as if he can control himself no longer. He glances at Dauoodaset. When Dauoodaset only glares at him, he quickly turns back to me. "I don't know what you got planned, but just listen to me. You had me believing you liked me. You did, didn't you? So you suckered me into that just to get me here? Whoever you are, you got no right to be screwing around with people's lives like this!"

Dauoodaset can stand his shouting at me no longer. He snatches from his waist pouch a long strip of leather. He wraps one end around each hand and yanks it tight. David stares at him. He is quick to get back the terror in his eyes.

He jumps to his feet, but Dauoodaset is after him before he has a chance to go far. He whips his arms over David's head and draws the leather strip tight across his chest, tripping him with his foot to the ground. David groans in pain. He fights to get free. But he is no match for Dauoodaset. Dauoodaset forces his knee hard into his back, then ties his hands tight behind him.

He pulls him to his feet and pushes him back to the rocks by the fire. I am glad that it is over.

Blood is trickling down David's cheek to the corner of his mouth. He tries to wipe it into his shoulder. He looks at me with pain and disbelief in his eyes. I cannot look at him for long. I turn in silence and look around where I am standing.

This is not the way it was meant to be. I did not bring him here for this to happen. I must make him see that I am no longer of his world, that he is now a part of ours.

I go to him and wipe away blood from his face. "David," I whisper to him, "you must not struggle. It will do you no good. You must learn to listen and take us for who we are."

When I return to my place I ask Dauoodaset where there are the makings for hot drink. He shows me a pouch and from it I take some dried leaves. I will go to the canoe and get from it the knapsack and fresh water that I have brought with us.

I tell them both where I am going, and then I leave them alone together and make my way toward the shelf of rock and the beach beyond it. It will be good for them both to have me away from them.

On my return I stop just as I am in sight of the fire to see what is happening between them. They are standing across the fire from each other, each of them bare to the waist. Dauoodaset has untied the leather strip from David's wrists and made him take off some of his clothes.

The two are of the same age, fifteen years. They must know this when they look at each other.

Dauoodaset stands strong and tall, his black hair long to his shoulders, his muscles showing how hard they are. Red ochre is thick over his body. His face tells of his hatred for those who would starve his people and chase them with guns.

David is standing with a body that is stiff and full of fright. His arms are folded about him. The air from the saltwater makes him shiver and turns his white skin red with the cold.

"Ashei," Dauoodaset says to him.

David stares at him with a mind that is dazed.

"Dauoodaset calls you sickly," I tell him as I come close to where they are.

David's head turns quickly to me. He stares into my eyes, anger rising again through his fear. His arms drop to his sides. His hands tighten into fists. He stands stiff, his muscles tense, trying to stop his shivering. His body is stronger than I thought it would be. Dauoodaset, too, sees this. But, Dauoodaset says to me, there are no scars like those of a hunter and man of the woods.

"Is this his crazy way to make fun of me?" David says, still staring at me.

I tell him no, but it is not enough. He has too much anger in him to understand the ways of my people. "Cover your body again. Warm yourself with the fire."

He is slow to do it. He tries to make it look as if the cold does not bother him. There is a pride in who he is that I have not seen before.

When I have put some water to boil, we sit again by the fire. There is much for me to talk about with Dauoodaset.

We talk of the future and how it will be with us, how there will be many that will be born to us and who will grow and spread about this island, and their children after them. We will make a new beginning for our people.

When the water begins to bubble I add to it the leaves that I took from Dauoodaset's pouch. It makes a strong drink that warms us well. At first Dauoodaset thinks it odd to be drinking from such a vessel as we have brought. I bring to his memory how by the great lake our fathers used such things left for us by the whitemen. He reminds me how after the killings we cast them away and went back to our own ways.

I tell David all of what we speak. I say how it cannot be that way again, that he must see us as we are, and he must tell others they have to learn to share this island with us. The food of the waters about this island is not for his people alone.

He seems to listen to what I say, but perhaps he is thinking only of a time when he will return to his home.

I bring out now the food that I have brought — biscuits and raisins and chocolate. Dauoodaset takes from a pouch scraps of dried caribou and offers it to us. I take it eagerly, for I have longed for caribou meat for many days. David shakes his head and will not take any of it.

Dauoodaset is hurt. It is not our way not to share in what has been offered. I tell David this, but it is of no use. He sees Dauoodaset forcing himself to eat what I have brought, and still he does not show any kindness toward him.

Why does he act this way? He no longer fears for his life. Can there be jealousy still in his heart?

"I trusted you," he says, and now I know that it is so.

"But can you not see that I had to do this for my people? And do you not feel proud that it is you alone who have seen us as we are?"

"It's a mad hoax, that's all it is. Some crazy scheme . . . "

"No, David, it is not so. You must believe that."

"I don't know what to believe."

"Believe what you know to be right. That is all."

He looks at me in a way that makes me want to hold him against me and make his doubts go away. But it can be to Dauoodaset alone that I can show such affection. Dauoodaset would not understand whiteman's ways such as that.

"My duty is to my people," I say to David. "It must be as friends that we share with one another."

I stop now my speaking to him. He needs time to think about all that I have said and know that it is true.

Dauoodaset and I have many things to do. We must make together a place of shelter. Not far from the fire are slender trees that we can cut and trim for poles and nearby are birch whose bark will make a covering around the poles. The ax I have brought in the knapsack with the food will make quick work.

We keep watch on David. He must stay with us until he understands the ways of my people. He is the one who will tell others of the truth of a new beginning for us. He must know the great importance of his task.

He is looking long and hard at the way we work. Dauoodaset cuts many poles and cleans them of branches. He sharpens them at the ends and drives them into the mossy ground. The tops of the poles come together to make the frame for our shelter. They must be tied together where they meet. This I try to do, but David can see I have not the steadiness that I need to climb on Dauoodaset's shoulders.

I ask him if he will help us. He is slow to answer, but after a while he rises from where he has been sitting all the time by the fire. He walks slowly to us and takes the leather strip from my hands. He looks then at Dauoodaset. He must be thinking of how Dauoodaset chased him with such a strip. But in his hands now it is not a weapon. There is no look in his eyes that would say he wants to use it for one.

He hands the strip to Dauoodaset and points to the top of the poles. He is saying that he wants Dauoodaset to get on his shoulders, that he will be the one to do the hardest work. There is for a time almost laughter on Dauoodaset's face. And when David stoops down low, he is slow to do as he wants. But then, like a hunter edging onto thin ice, he climbs upon his shoulders. David straightens up slowly, but does not stumble. His face is twisted with the strain of Dauoodaset's weight. Dauoodaset is quick to tie the poles together and David is quick to let him back down to the ground.

There is between them now a different look. There is pride in each of their faces, one as strong as the other.

David sits by the fire again. But after a time he comes to where we are cutting birch bark and takes from his jeans a pocketknife. Dauoodaset draws back when he sees the blade. David smiles a little, and then shows how quick it cuts away the sheets of bark that we have been struggling to get from the tree. After a while of watching him, Dauoodaset is eager to try for himself.

It is not long before we have the bark woven in layers around the poles, with other poles placed against it to help hold it together. Now we have a place of shelter, one that will protect us until the time we will build a bigger and stronger one.

After all our work it is good to rest by the fire. We sit about and talk of what we can cook for a meal. I tell David he will need to eat well to build his strength for the journey back to his home. He says nothing, but in the look that he gives us there is much relief. When Dauoodaset talks eagerly of places about the shore where there are mussels, David is anxious for me to tell him what he said.

It is good to see a bit of the David that I knew before. There is in him now a spirit that I thought I would not see again. When I tell him of the mussels his lips move with hunger and there is a look of pleasure straining to show on his face.

"Good," he says, but I can tell he means more than that.

Dauoodaset smiles at him and talks of other food we can have from about this island. He points to David and then to his bow and arrows. He says in our language that he can show him how to be a sharp hunter and man of the woods. I tell David what Dauoodaset has said.

David's reaction is not strong, but it is enough for me to know he is thinking how it could be true what Dauoodaset says, how together they would make great hunters. Dauoodaset sees it too and is pleased.

"Good," David says, and this time it sounds like it is from his heart.

There is good feeling between us all.

"Let us make the meal. Our hunger can wait no longer," I tell them, smiling. "Dauoodaset will bring us mussels. We will build up the fire and heat water to boil them. A feast is what we will make."

Soon Dauoodaset is gone to the shore and David is gathering up more wood for the fire. I have found good stones for cooking. They will hold much heat and be quick to boil the water. We will need more than one pot for cooking. We can make ones of birch skin and use the metal one that I have brought in the knapsack.

I go about my work, except to glance at David to see that he is still nearby. From one side, with his face smeared red with dried blood, he looks like one of my people.

"Nancy," he says quietly when he is near me by the fire, "I know you feel a lot more for me than this."

He talks to me as if there is still some of the girl that he

139

knew before. There is in his voice that liking he had for me.

I cannot look at him. It would not be good for either of us.

"I still like you a lot," he says.

I will not listen to him. I try to push back one of the cooking stones with a stick. The fire burns my hand.

I drop the flaming stick and put my hand to my mouth.

I feel fire on me! The fur of my legging has caught fire from the stick I dropped. There is flame running about my leg!

Before I can cry to Dauoodaset for help, David has pushed me to the ground and is smothering the flame with his own body.

The fire is gone. We are on the ground together, David kneeling over me. The flame did not burn me, only part of my legging. There is only the foul smell of the burnt fur.

No words are spoken between us. I look at him and he knows that I am thankful. He stares at me and I do not look away.

"Shanawdithit will always be grateful," I tell him.

He is still staring into my eyes.

Then from his neck falls something that makes my breath stop and my eyes stare without belief. It is a bone piece — the one that I gave to Dauoodaset when he left the great lake to go to the new land with his family! It hangs loose on a strip of leather, its coloring of red ochre pale and worn.

David sees my surprise. I cannot speak. I have no words to explain to him all that the bone piece means to me.

David stands up and takes it from about his neck. I rise too from the ground and stand in front of him. He puts the leather strip over my head and lets the bone piece fall against my body furs. I feel in me a warmness I have not felt since I have known him.

He goes then away from me, to the rocks where we were sitting before.

Suddenly his head jerks back and his eyes widen, as if he is surprised by something behind me.

Before I can turn, a hand is tight against my mouth! My head is locked against an arm!

I am trying to scream to Dauoodaset, but no sound can get out. My heart is jumping madly!

"I got her. They won't hurt you now," a man's voice says gruffly to David.

I can see no face, only the long point of the gun he holds in his other hand. Where has he come from? Why is he here?

I fight to get myself free from him. I try to bite his hand, but it is no use. Nothing I do can get me away from him.

"Hold still!" he yells at me.

Now his dirty hand is harder against my mouth. I am sick with anger.

"Where you come from?" he says to David. "Down the shore? I thought it was only the two of us in this bay. You see my brother? I knowed he came over to this island. I heard his gun and I seen his boat where it come ashore."

He is a whiteman, a brother of the one who shot at Dauoodaset. This cannot be. They cannot do this to us again.

"She has done nothing to you," David says to him. "Let her go."

"Have you no sense? They steal our gear and rob our nets. Bloody red thieves. Like animals they are."

I want to shut my ears to this. He is talking as if we are savages. It is his kind who are the savages. Our pain means nothing to them.

"Don't hurt her," David says to him in a voice that is not strong enough.

I stare at David. Why can he not make him see that we mean no harm to them, that all we want is our rightful share of this island? Is he thinking the fellow is a long-ago relative of his people?

Suddenly, from the trees nearest the shore, Dauoodaset can be seen! He stands rigid, his eyes raging at the devil who still has me held so I cannot move. Dauoodaset shouts at him words he does not understand.

Now Dauoodaset walks slowly toward us. His eyes are fixed on that devil. His rage is for what he is doing to me.

"Let her go, you fool!" David shouts.

The words are gone without notice, and now it is too late. Dauoodaset is coming fast toward us, ready to tear that whiteman devil from me.

"Stop him, use the ax!" he shouts at David.

"Let her go!" David screams back at him.

David starts to run, to get to us before Dauoodaset can. But it is too late. The devil has pushed me to the ground. His gun is in the air.

A crack like thunder!

My screaming cuts the air louder than the noise of any gun!

Dauoodaset slumps to the ground.

His body lies crumpled next to the fire like it was when first I came to him. When I look at him I know he will not rise again. His life is gone from this land.

I am running now as fast as I can away from that whiteman devil. I do not care if he shoots me in the back. I must run.

I am Shanawdithit. I am the last of my people.

I glance back over my shoulder. I see David throw himself at the devil, sending the gun flying from his hands. Now he is on top of him on the ground, hitting him wildly with his fists.

That picture of David travels with me as I run.

I make it to the edge of the woods. I must get to where Dauoodaset's canoe lies upon the shore. I run through the woods until I am far away from them. Then I turn in the direction that will bring me to the shore. I do not stop even though the branches of the trees cut across my arms when I hold them up to shield my face. The rocks and sticks cut into my feet and once I stumble and trip across a fallen tree.

At last I break out of the woods to the shore. I look along the shoreline, but the land turns out to a point and I cannot tell how far I have to go beyond it.

I cannot lose time. I am splashing now along the water's edge. The salt burns into the cuts on my feet. I stop only when I get to the point.

From there I can see the canoe. There is no one in sight anywhere around me. I see only the last smoke of Dauoodaset's fire.

I race the rest of the way to the canoe. I throw the rocks from it and empty it of water. As quickly as I can, I return a few of the rocks to their place. The moss that was there must have washed away. I have no time to gather more. I push the canoe into the water, and kneeling now on the rocks, I push it with the paddle away from the shore. Then, with all the strength I have left, I paddle away.

Only when I am safely out of the range of guns do I slow my stroke. Now there is the time to think of all that has happened. I have to stop.

Tears fall down my face. I do not wipe them away, but start my paddling again.

Ahead of me there is open water. It is calm now, but I do not know how long it will last.

After my people first came to the waters about this island others call Newfoundland, the men paddled out in canoes long distances to where the seabirds nested in thousands, to be with those creatures and to feed on their eggs.

I see birds in the sky ahead of me. They will lead me there. I will go there now, the first woman of my people to do it.

I must go to the most distant land that my people have gone to before. The spirits of my people fly with me as I go. I am singing their songs, loud to the wind that begins to rise in heavy gusts about the canoe.

I am Shanawdithit, the last of my people.

David

David had attacked him with the savageness of a wild animal defending its territory. He was out to kill him if he had to, no matter who he was.

He was on top of him, pounding his fists into his face before the fellow realized what had happened. He struck frantically at David, sending him backward to the ground near the gun. David grabbed it by the barrel and stood up. He swung it with all his strength. The butt caught the man in the shoulder just as he was on his feet and drove him back to his knees. A second swing struck him in the side of the head. He dropped down senseless.

David threw the gun to the ground and looked around him.

"Nancy!" he called. "Shanawdithit!"

He caught a glimpse of her just as she disappeared into the woods. He took off after her.

In the woods he lost sight of her and had to stop, his heart pounding, to listen for the far-off sound of branches breaking under her feet.

Eventually he broke out to the shoreline. He rushed about until he saw traces of her footprints heading toward a point of land. He raced to it.

Once there, he came to a sudden stop.

In the distance off from shore was a canoe like the ones he had seen in books on the Beothuks. She was paddling it straight out to the open sea.

"Shanawdithit!" he called, running now along the shore to where the canoe must have entered the water.

"Shanawdithit!"

She did not turn when he called. The high curves of the canoe hid all but the steady stroke of her paddling.

David stood up to his knees in the saltwater, calling her again and again until he knew there was no hope of her coming back to him.

The canoe gradually grew fainter, not from the distance, but as if it took the color and shape of the sea all about it. And then there was no more of it, no trace of it.

She had left him alone, standing in the saltwater, staring helplessly out to the sea, empty except for seabirds flying far, far off from shore.

There was nothing he could do but go back the way he had come. He stood for a long time on the point of land.

He thought of all that had happened. Most of all he thought of Shanawdithit and how she was the last of her people.

All the way back through the woods he was shivering with the cold from his wet clothes and with the fear of how he would deal with what he had left by the fire.

He broke out from the woods. He stopped.

There was no fire. No sign of there ever being a fire! And no sign of there ever being anyone there!

He walked about in a daze, his arms around himself. How could this be?

He stood near the spot where he had beaten the fellow to the ground. It was overgrown with bushes. Thick grass covered the ground where the fire had been. He examined the trees around for signs of bark being stripped away. There were none.

He sat on the rocks where they had sat together. Tears began to fill his eyes.

He stayed there for a long time shivering, trying to make sense of it.

He walked about again, aimlessly searching for clues as to what had happened. He could find none.

Drifting away from the site, he climbed the rock shelf and stood up and looked back to where he had first seen them together.

"Shanawdithit!" he shouted. "Dauoodaset!"

He waited and waited. Then he turned away and looked along the beach to where his canoe was lying half in the water and half out.

He turned back quickly and called again. There was nothing. He sat down on the rock and stared at where the fire had been.

He sat there for a long time, his reddened hands to his mouth, blowing his breath into them to keep away the cold.

When he could stand it no longer, he walked along the beach to the canoe. And now that the wind had died away, he was gone from the island, back to his home and his family.

About the Author

KEVIN MAJOR's first novel, *Hold Fast*, received three major Canadian book awards, was named to the Hans Christian Andersen List, and was chosen as a Best Book of 1980 by *School Library Journal*. His second novel, *Far from Shore*, was the winner of the Canadian Young Adult Book Award and was chosen as a Best Book of 1981 by *School Library Journal*. Kevin Major has also written *Thirty-six Exposures* and *Dear Bruce Springsteen*.

The author lives with his wife and two children in Newfoundland.